LOVE

IS THE

HIGHER
LAW

LOVE
IS THE
HIGHER
LAW

david

levithan

Alfred A. Knopf

New York

THIS IS A BORZOI BOOK PUBLISHED BY ALFRED A. KNOPF

Copyright © 2009 by David Levithan

Grateful acknowledgment is made to Cindy Bullens for permission to reprint an excerpt
from her song "Better Than I've Ever Been."

Visit us on the Web! www.randomhouse.com/teens

Educators and librarians, for a variety of teaching tools, visit us at
www.randomhouse.com/teachers

The Library of Congress has cataloged the hardcover edition of this work as follows:
Levithan, David.
Love is the higher law / David Levithan.
p. cm.
Summary: Three New York City teens express their reactions to the bombing of the
World Trade Center on September 11, 2001, and its impact on their lives and the world.
ISBN 978-0-375-83468-4 (trade) — ISBN 978-0-375-93468-1 (lib. bdg.) —
ISBN 978-0-375-89360-5 (e-book)
[1. September 11 Terrorist Attacks, 2001—Fiction. 2. Interpersonal relations—Fiction.
3. Homosexuality—Fiction. 4. World politics—1995–2005—Fiction.
5. New York (N.Y.)—Fiction.] I. Title.
PZ7.L5798Lov 2009 [Fic]—dc22 2008040886

ISBN 978-0-375-83469-1 (tr. pbk.) 6/11
462075 01
Printed in the United States of America
August 2010
10 9 8 7 6 5 4 3 2

First Trade Paperback Edition

To Craig Walker
(who was next to me on 9/11)

and

To Eliot Schrefer
(who was across the table when
I wrote most of this book)

WHAT JUST HAPPENED

(Part One)

MY FIRST THOUGHT
Claire

My first thought is: *My mother is dead.*

When Mrs. Shields, the school secretary, shows up so gravely in the doorway and gestures for Mrs. Otis to come over to her, I am sure that my mother has died, that I am now going to have to pack up my books and go to Sammy's school and collect him and tell him that Mom is dead and I'm all he has now and somehow we'll get by. I am so sure that something is wrong, incredibly wrong, and I can't imagine what else it could be. I am already gathering my books as Mrs. Shields whispers to Mrs. Otis. I see Mrs. Otis nod, distressed, and then Mrs. Shields disappears back into the hall. I sit up straighter, waiting for Mrs. Otis to look at me, to say my name. But instead she looks at all of us and says, "Class, a plane has hit the World Trade Center."

Katie Johnson gasps. Other kids start talking.

I am blank.

And then Mrs. Otis asks, "Do any of you have parents working in the World Trade Center?"

We look around. No. But Teresa says that Jill Breslin, who's in one of the other senior English classes, has a father who works there. I think of our apartment, only ten blocks away from the towers. I know my mother isn't home. I know she left with me and Sammy this morning and continued uptown to her office. But suddenly I'm wondering: *What if she forgot something? What if she went back to the apartment? What if she took the subway down to Chambers Street, underneath the towers?*

I've gone from being sure she's dead to being unsure she's alive, and that's much scarier, because it almost feels rational.

Mrs. Otis informed us on the first day of school that there would be no cell phone usage tolerated in class, but now it's the fifth day of school and there's nothing she can do. She's trying to hold it together, but she's as confused as we are. Cell phones are ringing, and all these kids are telling their parents they're okay, we're all okay—our school is a good thirty blocks north of the Trade Center. Abby Winter's mom starts telling her what the news is saying, and then she tells it to the rest of us: "The plane hit around the ninetieth floor. The building's still standing, and people are evacuating. Firemen are going up. The other tower looks like it's okay. . . ."

My friend Randy spots a TV in the back of the class, but when he tries it out, all we get is static. I know Randy has a phone and I ask him if I can use it. I try calling Mom's office, but nobody picks up. I leave a message on the answering machine, telling her I'm okay.

The principal gets on the PA and says that all the classes have been informed of the "situation downtown," and that if there are any "concerned students," they should come to the guidance

4

suite. We all know what he means by *concerned students*—he means if your parents are there.

We're not a big school. There are only about seventy kids in each grade. So I can't help imagining Jill Breslin down there in the guidance office, and a few other kids. Teresa's getting frantic now, saying she has to go see Jill. And it's not even like they're best friends. Mrs. Otis tries to calm her down, saying the guidance counselors will take care of it. And I think that kind of makes sense, since the guidance counselors are adults, but it also doesn't, because even if Teresa isn't best friends with Jill, she definitely knows Jill more than any of the guidance counselors do.

The thought of Jill Breslin in that guidance office makes me feel I should go to the lower school and see Sammy. I wonder if they've told the second graders what's happening, or if Mrs. Lawson is closing the blinds and giving them a spelling test.

Suddenly there's this big scream from the classroom next to ours—at least ten people yelling out. Mrs. Otis goes to the door connecting her room to Mr. Baker's, and about half our class follows, so we're there when she asks what's going on. But nobody needs to answer—Mr. Baker's gotten his TV to work, and it's not one but two towers that are burning, and they're saying on the TV that there was a second plane, that the towers are under attack, and seeing it erases any premonitions I might have had, because even if I felt something was wrong, I never would have pictured this. This isn't even something I've feared, because I never knew it was a possibility. Kids are crying now, both in Mr. Baker's class and in my class, and we're looking at each other like

5

What do we do? and the principal is on the PA again telling everyone to remain calm, which only makes it worse. It's like the principal knows something he's not telling us, and the TV is saying that people are jumping, and Teresa just loses it completely, and we're all thinking about Jill and who knows who else, and people are trying to call their parents on their cell phones, but now all the lines are busy, or maybe they've stopped working, and I don't even have a cell phone and neither does my mother. I just want to get Sammy and go home.

All of our class is in Mr. Baker's room now—it's practically the whole twelfth grade. Mrs. Otis and Mr. Baker are in the front, talking to each other, and then Mrs. Otis heads to the office to see what's going on. Randy offers his phone to me again, but says it's not really working, although maybe it will work for me. It doesn't, and I don't know what else I can do, except I realize now I should've given my mom Randy's number. The TV is showing people downtown running away. I tell Randy I have to get my brother, and saying it to him makes it mean I'm going to do it.

I go up to Mr. Baker and say my brother's in the lower school, in second grade, and I have to go get him. This girl Marisol hears me and says her sister's over there, too, in first grade, and is probably really scared. Mr. Baker says nobody is supposed to leave the school, but we tell him we're only going across the street, and we must sound really desperate, because he looks at us and says it's fine, as long as we come straight back.

I don't know Marisol at all—she's new to the school, and the only reason I remember her name is because when it was called in attendance on the first day, I thought it was a pretty name. I take her to the side door, because I'm afraid someone from the office will stop us if we try the main door.

"I can't believe this is happening," Marisol says.

"I know," I say.

But we have no idea until we're out the door and onto Sixth Avenue. We don't even see it at first—we just see everyone else looking up, and then we turn to look back at what they're seeing. The towers are burning and people are cupping their hands over their eyes and staring straight at it. Shaking their heads or crying. Looking at each other in disbelief. Total strangers are talking to each other, saying "Oh my Lord" and "I never thought . . ." And then there are the people—this steady flow of people—coming from downtown. These are the people we were seeing on the TV just a few minutes ago, escaping what just happened. Some of them are covered in what looks like heavy dust, chalk almost, and others are just ragged from getting away. Strangers are coming up to them and asking if they're okay, if they need any help. One guy has opened up his shoe store and is giving out sneakers to women in heels. Just giving them away.

Marisol grabs my hand, and I let her. We're about to cross the street when we hear a siren—an ambulance heading north. There should be more ambulances coming from downtown, I think. It's scary that there's just one.

Marisol is crying now, and she takes her hand from mine so she can wipe her eyes.

"Sorry," she says.

There's a guard at the lower school, and even though we tell him we're here to get Marisol's sister and my brother, he makes us sign in and get a pass. I show Marisol where her sister's room is, then say goodbye. We're far from the only visitors—there are moms and dads coming to pick up their kids, and I have to admit that I'm hoping our mom will be one of them. I know she'd come for Sammy first.

I want her to be here already. Because that would mean she's definitely alive.

I get to the classroom and Mom is nowhere to be found. There's no TV, but the kids are definitely aware that something bad is happening, because parents keep arriving, and while nobody wants to say how bad it is, there's no way to pretend it's a normal day.

Sammy's teacher, Mrs. Lawson, is the same teacher I had for second grade. "Are you here for Sammy?" she asks, and I say yes. Then I realize she's asking if I'm going to take Sammy away, and I tell her that we live downtown, so there's nowhere for us to go. I've never in my life said those words before. *There's nowhere for us to go.* I feel it. I ask Mrs. Lawson if she needs any help.

I need to stay here. I need to stay close to Sammy.

"I'd love that," she says. She gestures toward the desks. "We were drawing flowers. Maybe if you could go around and help them. At least until everything's straightened out."

8

My first stop is Sammy, who gives me a big hug and asks me if we're going home like Lucas is.

"Not yet," I tell him. "Let's do some drawing first."

"Is Mommy coming?"

"Yes," I say. "She's on her way."

The kids' desks are pushed together so that each set of six makes a tabletop. Sammy's best friend, Spencer, is at the same tabletop as him, and he asks me if *his* mommy is coming. I tell him I think so.

"Now, let's see those flowers," I say.

Since it's the first full week of school, all of the supplies are brand-new. The crayons are unbroken; some of them even have points. The pencils are newly sharpened, the erasers bright pink. I can't help but think, *This was supposed to be a good day.* I feel nostalgia for an hour ago, when Sammy and I were walking from the subway stop, taking in the sunny weather, making jokes about SpongeBob SquarePants.

"Look at mine!" the girl next to me demands, and I compliment her on her flower (even if it looks more like an elephant than a tulip) and tell her to draw more.

A few more parents make it to the class, and each time one appears in the doorway, half the class turns, including me. The kid whose parent has arrived jumps up and runs over. The rest of us go back to what we're doing.

Spencer proudly holds up his paper for me to see.

"Do you like it?" he asks.

I see a gray blob with green highlights.

"It's fantastic," I tell him.

"Do you know what it is?"

I'm pretty sure it's not a flower.

"An alien?" I ask.

His face falls a little. "No."

"A rhinoceros."

His face falls further. "No."

I am never going to guess.

"What is it?" I ask.

"*You*," he says. "I drew *you*."

Sammy laughs, and I tell Spencer extra loud that I love it. Maybe Spencer's nailed it—maybe that's actually what I look like right now.

Since there's no TV, the parents are the only way we find out news. And when they stop coming—when there are only about ten kids left in the classroom—Mrs. Lawson leaves for a second so she can see what's going on. Spencer asks me to tell the class a story, and since I can't think of one off the top of my head, I grab the nearest book and tell them about a dog Cinderella. I try to focus on the story, not on the door and who might walk through it, because I know the kids are trying to follow my lead. We can hear more sirens on the street outside.

Mrs. Lawson comes back and looks stricken. I finish the book and get the kids going on a new drawing project—pumpkin carriages—and go over to her for the update. She tells me they don't know how many people were in the towers—it could be as high as twenty-five thousand, although it's probably more like ten thousand. And there is another plane that hit the Pentagon. There could be more. Nobody knows.

She tells me this in a whisper. Then we walk back over to the kids and try to gather enough orange crayons from the other tables so they can all draw pumpkins. The world is falling apart, and this is what we have to offer.

Spencer's mom arrives and says it took her ages to get to the school from uptown, since everything has shut down. She says that Sammy and I can come back with her to the Upper East Side. But that's so far away, and I'm worried that if the phones stay down, there will be no way for Mom to find us. I have to believe she's going to be here any minute. Plus, I don't want to leave Mrs. Lawson alone. So Sammy and I say goodbye to Spencer, and this is the point—now that his mom is here—that Spencer begins to cry, loudly protesting that he doesn't want to leave, that school's not over yet. He's crying about the wrong thing, and I find myself almost jealous of that.

It takes all of his mom's promises for Spencer to be persuaded—Sammy can come over later; Daddy will be home from work when they get back; they can have dessert before dinner tonight. Mrs. Lawson and I are so enthusiastic about each of these things that I half expect the other kids to chime in with their own tears, to see what rewards they'll get. I hope they won't, because I don't think Mrs. Lawson and I could take it.

Eventually Spencer leaves, with his mom promising to keep calling my mom's office until she gets through. We are about to resume our carriage drawing when an announcement comes on the PA saying that all teachers and their classes should pack up their things and report to the gymnasium. We are going to be leaving the building.

Neither Mrs. Lawson nor I know why this is happening or what it means. Since the weather is so summery, there isn't much bundling up to be done.

In the gymnasium, the principal gently announces that one of the towers has fallen and people are being encouraged to move north of Fourteenth Street. Because of this, the administrators have decided to evacuate the building and move everyone to another school, on Seventeenth Street. It's only a twelve-block walk, and everyone is going to stick together. The school secretaries will stay in the office to field calls, and the guard will stay in the main hallway, so if any parent or guardian comes by, he or she will be redirected to the new school. He also adds that transportation and communication in the city are extremely difficult at the moment, so if our parents haven't arrived or called, it is probably not for a lack of trying.

I am still upset with my mother, though. And scared.

If you ever lose me, I remember her saying when I was little and we'd go to a department store, *just let one of the salesladies know, and they will take you to where I can find you.* Even though I'm seventeen, I guess I still thought this would always be true—that there would always be that lost-and-found, and not the lost-and-still-lost that I am now trapped inside.

The principal does not ask if anyone has any questions. He tells the classes to line up behind their teachers and starts releasing them, oldest to youngest, into the hallway and out the front door. Each teacher has been assigned another adult—a custodian or an aide or a volunteer parent—to help keep everything in order. I look over to the first graders and see that Marisol is there with her sister. There's no way that we're going back to the high school building, and nobody seems to think it's odd that we're here. We catch each other's eye, and I almost wave. We have a kinship now, as thin as a thread, but permanent.

One of the towers has fallen. When it's our turn to leave, it's like something in me is finally willing to listen, and suddenly I understand what it means. The tower doesn't exist anymore. Something I've seen my entire life—something so much larger than my entire life—is gone. That is my first reaction. And then I think about all the people inside. There must have been people inside.

When we get to Sixth Avenue, I feel like I'm in one of those myths where the one thing the woman can't do is turn around and see what's behind her. I am holding Sammy's hand and this girl Lizzie's hand, following Mrs. Lawson, and all I can think is, *Don't look back.* If I turn around, Sammy and Lizzie will also turn around. If I turn around, they will see it. If I turn around, I may disintegrate.

The street is jammed with people walking north. Some were clearly close to the towers, since the smoke and the dust cling to their skin and their clothes.

"What happened to them?" Sammy asks, and I don't know what to say. I can't even think of a good lie. So I treat it like he's asked a different question and tell him we're almost there, even though we still have five blocks to go. I wish I was still at the age when I needed explanations, and would receive better versions than the truth whenever I asked.

The only time I've seen this many people on Sixth Avenue has been for the Halloween Parade. I am amazed at how respectful everyone is. There are skyscrapers collapsing behind us, and nobody is pushing, nobody is yelling. When people see we're a school group, they're careful not to separate us. Stores are not only giving away sneakers, but some are handing out water to people who need it. You'd think they'd take advantage and raise the price. But no. That's not what happens.

I am looking everywhere for familiar faces. There's a small line of people moving against the march, weaving their way downtown. There's no mistaking their purpose as they push forward. Every single one of them has a reason. It must be someone they love. Or a desire to help.

Don't look back, I remind myself. *Don't look back.*

I hear my name called out—"*Claire!*"—then Sammy's. He's quicker to react.

"Mom!" he yells. He stops walking, pulling me and Lizzie to a halt. And then she's running over, and Sammy lets go of me, and it's okay because Mom is right there, and we're slowing up the line, and Mrs. Lawson is getting farther ahead, so my first words to Mom are "We have to keep walking." She doesn't question this. She is crying to see us, and this is the first time I've ever seen her crying to see us, and she's practically carrying

Sammy even though he's too big to carry anymore, and she's telling us how happy she is to have found us, and how hard it was. She had to walk all the way from Eighty-ninth Street on the East Side because she had a meeting there, and as soon as she can, she's going to buy all of us cell phones. And what I want to shout is *I thought you were dead,* but not in front of Sammy or poor Lizzie, who I don't even know, whose parents still aren't here. I explain to Mom why we're walking north; she nods, and I get a good look at her—she's holding it together, too, and I want to tell her she doesn't have to do that for me, because I might not be able to do it for her. I can tell she's also trying not to look back, but she does it—she looks over her shoulder—and the tears won't leave her eyes.

"It's so horrible," she says. "I hope you didn't see . . ."

And I think, *What didn't I see?*

Later that night, after Sammy is asleep, we piece it together, mapping out our day against the news. We are in an apartment on Eighteenth Street where Mom's friends Ted and Lia live. I was friends with their daughter, Rana, when I was little, but Rana is away at college now. Mom, Ted, Lia, and I watch CNN at midnight as they give us the chronology of what happened.

While I was holding Sammy's hand and Lizzie's hand, while we were following Mrs. Lawson, the second tower fell. We were too far away to hear it or to feel the ground shake. If you weren't watching—if you hadn't turned back to look—there was no way to know. You could imagine they were both still there.

15

Just in the same way we imagine our own apartment is there, waiting for us, untouched. We're not allowed to go home.

"We are not supposed to comprehend something like this," my mother says to me as we watch the latest update before she heads to bed. It's a sentence that I keep repeating to myself. I even take solace in it. I cannot comprehend. I don't want to comprehend. Instead I will try to remember what matters. I will do this as I wonder what happens next.

Even though they tell me to sleep, I watch the news all night.

I don't want to know anything, and I want to know it all.

WAKE UP, IT'S OVER
Jasper

I missed the whole goddamn thing. Slept late, woke up to the phone ringing, was completely oblivious. In fact, I was pissed that the phone was ringing, because it was before noon, and it was the house line, which meant it probably wasn't for me. I had two weeks before I had to go back to school, and I'd been planning to spend those two weeks sleeping. And when I wasn't sleeping, I was planning to nap. So I would've had the machine pick it up, only I'd unplugged the machine a couple of nights before when someone was leaving a message that I couldn't deal with—something about getting out the vote, blah blah blah— and the only way I could think to shut it up was to pull out the plug. I was maybe a little drunk at the time, so it made sense then. But now the phone was ringing for the eleventh time and I realized if it was important and I didn't get it, my parents would find out and I'd be wading knee-deep in the shit. So I stumbled out of bed in my boxers and yelled at the phone to hold on, I was coming.

It was still ringing when I got there, and I was a little surprised when I picked it up and said hello and my mom started saying thank God it was me, thank God I was okay. My first reaction was, what the fuck have the neighbors been telling her, and did they really call Korea to let her know I was drinking so much? And then my father was on the phone, too, and he was saying they were watching CNN and it was just terrible, completely terrible, and it had taken forever for them to get through. I had to say I had no idea what he was talking about, and then, only then, did he say, "Did we wake you?" And I wasn't going to lie—I said, yeah, they had, so this whole phone call wasn't making much sense to me, and that's when he told me the World Trade Center was gone—that's how he said it, "The World Trade Center is gone," and I honestly thought, *Does he mean Grandma?* because that's why he and Mom were in Korea in the first place, but obviously I was wrong on that count, because Grandma was fine, it was just all these other people who were dead.

As he was telling me this, I walked over to the window, and, Jesus, even from Park Slope you could see that something completely hellish had happened. There was all this smoke billowing up from downtown. And the Twin Towers were nowhere to be found.

"Holy shit," I said. "I mean, holy shit."

This was probably the first time I'd ever cursed while talking to my parents, but they didn't reprimand me. Mom was saying she wished she could be with me, that they would try to get home on the first available plane. I asked them what else was going on in the city, and my dad couldn't resist it, he said, "For once in your life, turn on the news." So I took the phone into the other room and turned on the TV, and it was amazing to see what was going on practically next door to me, and it was totally surreal that I'd slept through it all. My parents were telling me to go to the grocery and stock up on water and canned goods, like Brooklyn was going to be under siege at any minute. I said yes to everything they said, and then when my mother started crying, I told her I was going to be fine, that I knew how to take care of myself, which is why they'd left me alone here in the first place. This made her cry even more, the idea of me being left alone, and I assured her I still had a lot of friends who hadn't headed back to college yet, and if I needed somewhere to go, there were plenty of places I could crash. When that wasn't enough, I even said I'd take my cell phone with me so she could reach me whenever. This made her quiet down a little, and my father said that it was probably time for them to go, and that I shouldn't hesitate to call them if anything went wrong. For one stupefying moment he was quiet, and I actually thought he was going to say he loved me or something out of control like that. But as usual, he left that to Mom, who—also as usual—overcompensated, although in a situation like this, when your only son is almost seven thousand miles away from you and his city's under terrorist attack, I guess there's no such thing as overdoing it.

After I hung up, I sat on the couch in my boxers and watched more of the news, and all I could keep thinking was *Holy shit, holy shit.*

Once I'd gotten a grasp on what was going on and I was

reassured that terrorists wouldn't be storming over the Brooklyn Bridge anytime soon (or ramming a plane into it, for that matter), I decided to check my email. Lo and behold, it seemed that every single person I'd met in college, as well as a few I'd met before college, had emailed to see if I was okay. I guess they didn't know anyone else in New York City, or they didn't know that I lived in Brooklyn, or they were worried that I had gotten up early to check out the Observation Deck. (Thinking about the Observation Deck suddenly made me really sad. We always had relatives visiting from Korea, so we'd go and do the touristy things that most Brooklynites never do. I loved being up that high—in the clouds, sometimes—and I would always run to the east side of the building, even when I was older, to try to look out the window and see our house. I never saw it, but I swore I'd come close a couple of times.)

Some of the people who emailed me said I was in their prayers, and while that was a nice thing for them to say, I wanted to tell them their prayers could probably be redirected to more deserving people. But then I realized they had no idea whether I was dead or alive, so I basically responded to each and every one of them, saying I was fine, and that the city would be fine, and that I appreciated their concern. I didn't mention that I'd slept through the whole thing, and I definitely didn't mention that I was alone, because from the sound of some of the messages, I would've had a prayer circle on my doorstep in ten seconds flat, just to take care of me.

Even some of my high school friends, who were already

back at college, emailed me to say how weird it was to be away, hoping things weren't too crazy back home. I sent them back the same email saying I was okay, but I couldn't give them any real details, since all I knew was from TV, and it was probably the same thing they were watching in Chicago or Colorado or California.

There was one email from a guy named Peter, subject: RE: TONIGHT, and I blanked at first until I realized it was the guy I'd met at Mitchell's party Saturday night, who I was supposed to meet to go see *Hedwig and the Angry Inch* later in the day. He was a high school senior, which at first I wasn't sure about. But hell, I was only two years older and he was cute, so I'd said a date would be cool. Now he was saying:

> jasper—
>
> this is peter. from the party. with everything that's happening, i hope you're alright. i just got home from school—it was crazy. since it's looking like all the subways are out, i'm guessing our movie plans are off. i guess we can see how the week goes. i was really excited to see you (i know i'm not supposed to say that), but i promise i'll still be excited whenever we reschedule. if i have to walk across the bridge to get to your borough, so be it.
>
> again, i hope you and your family are okay.
>
> talk soon,
> peter

It was a little bit much for before a first date, but I emailed back to say, yeah, we'd reschedule. Normally I would have taken a day or two to respond, just so he wouldn't think I was eager or needy. But the whole notion that he might think I was dead or something made me figure it was better to write sooner rather than later.

Even though the news was saying phone service was spotty, my phone was working fine. I called Amanda, this girl who went to my school who also lived in Park Slope, and I asked her what was up, and she said she was going down to the hospital to give blood. I said, yeah, that was the right thing to do, and if she could wait a few minutes for me to put on some clothes, I'd go with her. She said sure, and I told her I'd pick her up.

In the shower, all my mind could do was wander back to *Holy shit*. I was afraid to check the news again, because what if this was just the beginning? What if there were more planes coming down, or bombs about to go off? I had to imagine Brooklyn was pretty safe. Except for the bridge, we were pretty much devoid of symbolic targets. It was hard to imagine terrorists getting excited about the Wonder Wheel on Coney Island. Still, even though I lived in Brooklyn, Manhattan was the reason I loved being from the city, and the idea of it disappearing was pretty dire. I knew there was no way to get there right now except by foot, and there was no reason to go, but part of me wanted to trek there anyway, just to help it out.

By the time I was fully awake and fully dressed, I had already seen the news loop around at least three times. I had seen the replays—so many replays, from so many angles—of the second plane hitting, of the towers falling, of the Pentagon burning. And I kept looking out the window. I kept seeing the smoke.

But nothing—I mean nothing—compared to stepping outside.

It was one of the things the news hadn't mentioned: the way the wind was blowing. East. So we were downwind from everything that had happened. The smoke was moving in our direction.

It wasn't like it blocked out the sun or anything. But it was there in the air, and the smell wasn't like any smoke I'd ever inhaled. This wasn't campfire smoke or even the smoke of a house that had burned down. No, this was much, much worse. It was like someone had strapped a tire under your nose and it was burning there. It came in waves—sometimes unbearably strong, other times thinned out. I honestly wondered whether I should've been wearing a breathing mask.

And then came the next thing, which is still the thing I remember the most, more than my parents' phone call, more than the images on TV. They were sitting in our front yard—the four-by-three-foot patch we call our front yard. Two sheets of paper. I only picked them up because I thought I might have dropped them; they didn't look like trash or flyers for the local Chinese restaurant (which seemed to be addicted to giving out flyers). At first I didn't get it—one sheet of paper was a printout from one of those old printers, the kind where the paper had holes on the edges so you could feed it through. It was a report from 1993 about a stock. Someone had initialed it on the bottom. The other piece of paper was a memorandum announcing someone's promotion. It was dated November 8, 1999. I recognized the name of the company immediately, since I'd just heard it mentioned so often on the news. Its headquarters was in the World Trade Center.

The planes hit the towers. When they did, thousands—maybe millions—of pieces of paper were knocked into the air. Others might have lifted when the towers fell. They were torn from their folders, their offices, their buildings, and they got caught in the wind and were carried. Some traveled only a block or two. Others fell into the East River. And some were scattered throughout Brooklyn.

A stock report and a human resources memorandum. Picking them up and reading them, I felt a sadness so deep that it will never really be gone. It was a sobering moment—sobering not because I was drunk, but because it felt like I was shifting into this new state of naked clarity. It was a higher state of sobriety, a painful state of sobriety, because the truth was suddenly unvarnished, making me feel unvarnished. Something as mundane as two sheets of paper from an office file could provide the final evidence of how vulnerable we are, how we live our lives not knowing how or when they will end. I had a sense then of how if we truly understood how many of the unimportant things we do will end up outliving us, we'd never be able to go on.

I wanted to go into our neighbor's yard, and the yard after

that, all the way down the block, down the street, to gather every piece of paper. As if they were all here to be found. As if a tower could be so easily reassembled.

Amanda called and asked where I was. I told her to hang on and went back inside to put the two pieces of paper in a safe place before I headed out again.

When I got to Amanda's, I told her about the papers, and she said lots of people were finding them. After the towers fell, Amanda went to Prospect Park, just to be near other people. Her mom was home and distraught, and her dad was stranded on the Upper West Side. She told me now how incredible it was—people just talking to each other, feeling this commonality that you want all human beings to have, but which never seems to happen in real life. I mean, even on a slow day, Prospect Park is a pretty friendly place; when I pointed this out to Amanda, she said it went beyond friendliness.

"It was kinship," she said.

"So suddenly you had all these new brothers and sisters?" I asked, maybe a little too sarcastic. In response, she hit my shoulder and told me it wasn't kinship like a family reunion, but something more intense than that.

Unsurprisingly, the line to give blood was around the block. It was, the newscasters kept saying, the one thing that the rest of us could do to help. So it looked like someone was giving out free tickets to a Rolling Stones/Tori Amos/Sonic Youth/Run DMC/Ani DiFranco/Backstreet Boys/Beastie Boys/Lou Reed/ Tony Bennett concert. Every possible Park Slope demographic was represented. But everyone's attitude was dialed down a notch—the hipsters didn't give a shit what they were wearing, the ghetto boys didn't strike any poses, and the carriage moms had left the carriages at home and weren't talking about their kids for once. People were talking about what had happened and where they'd been and who they knew who was there or might have been there. One guy was saying he'd had a meeting on the eightieth floor two days before. He said he wished he was a paramedic, so he could do something other than stand in line to give blood.

"Isn't it weird that we can, like, create phones that work anywhere, but we still can't make blood?" I asked Amanda, just as a way of making conversation. She just looked at me blankly. "Amanda?"

"Sorry," she said. "I'm not really here."

If Amanda and I weren't from the same area and going to the same college, I doubt we'd ever have been friends. It's not that we didn't like each other, it's just that the things we had in common were more geographical than attitudinal.

"Do you miss your parents?" she asked me now.

"Why—are you going to hire me a babysitter? If so, he better be hot."

I was just joking, but she got all snappish.

"I was only asking a question," she said.

"I was only asking a question back."

I couldn't believe that this, of all things, was going to upset her. But she was looking like I'd just put gum in her hair.

"Sorry," I backpedaled. "I mean, I don't really miss them. It wouldn't make it any different if they were here, right? They wouldn't have been able to, like, body block the Trade Center."

"That wasn't my point, and you know it."

So we stood there in silence for the next few minutes—or at least we were silent with each other. The woman in front of us started to talk to Amanda like they were old war buddies, and I kept looking back to see the line getting longer and longer. Finally we got within range of the Red Cross volunteer, who handed us a questionnaire.

"I'm sorry," he said, "but we're out of pencils. Maybe you can share?"

Amanda took a pen out of her bag and gave it to the woman in front of us. I started reading over the questionnaire. At first I thought, *I'm totally going to fail this*, because I had no idea what my blood type was. I didn't even know what the options were, except for type O negative, because that was the name of a band.

"Does blood type correspond to personality?" I asked Amanda. "Like, if I'm a type A personality . . ."

"Or type A asshole?"

"Point taken." *Type B bitch.*

I was starting to imagine this dying firefighter getting a pint of my blood and then, whammo, sitting upright in his hospital bed and crying, "I'm alive!" He and I would be in *People* magazine together, and maybe on the *Today* show, and he'd be really young and really cute, and maybe one night he'd say he had feelings for me, and I'd have to figure out if it was, like, narcissism or something if you slept with someone who had your blood inside of him, and then I'd decide it wasn't, and we'd be all happy together, and when people asked how we met, we'd say, "It's the craziest story. . . ."

Luckily, the questions got easier after the whole blood type thing. It was amazing how many diseases I'd never had. Then I got to the really interesting question:

Have you had any homosexual intercourse since 1980?

"Amanda?" I said. "Why do they want to know about my sex life?"

"AIDS?" she replied.

"But, yeah, they already asked about that. A couple of times. This is just about . . . intercourse."

"Maybe they just want to double-check?"

"Then why don't they ask you about *your* sex life? I've seen some of the guys you've slept with, and I wouldn't want any of their microbes in my arteries."

"Excuse me?"

"Except Simon. I'd take a little Simon in my blood."

"Can't you just let it rest for ten minutes?"

"And do what? Knit?"

The Earth Mother three people ahead of us turned around and gave me a nasty look—she had probably just put her knitting back in her bag in order to fill out the form. And actually, she wasn't the only one giving me a nasty look. It seemed like everybody was on the anti-Jasper bandwagon. Did the fact that

28

the World Trade Center had just been destroyed mean that I couldn't act normal with Amanda? I genuinely didn't see the point of looking somber and talking somber and thinking only somber thoughts. Who benefited from that? You have to imagine that the minute before that first plane hit, there were guys in the World Trade Center giving each other shit.

I left the intercourse question blank and finished my form. When the guy handing out the questionnaires passed by us again, I waved him down. He looked a little like my eighth-grade science teacher, with a comb-over and the kind of Eddie Bauer shirt that was supposed to simulate being on a safari for people who would never get as far as the Bronx Zoo.

"Hey," I said. "Can I ask you something?"

"Of course," he said.

I pointed out the question. "What's that about?"

"Oh, they need to know if you've had any homosexual intercourse."

He looked a little surprised that I of all people had asked the question. Which is what I love about American guys, especially straight ones. If you're not a flaming Filipino dancing queen, they never, ever expect the Asian guy to be asking about gay sex. They always figure you want to talk about math. Or the violin.

Normally in this situation, Amanda would be joining me in fighting the urge to laugh. But she was pretending like she was too busy writing everything she knew about heart disease in her family.

"Yeah," I said. "I figured that. But they mean unprotected sex, right? I mean, without a condom."

He shook his head. "No. It's really any gay sex."

I could tell that I wasn't the first guy to ask him about this. And I really wasn't in the mood to spell it out for him. I tried to keep it light.

"Let's say I have this friend," I said. "And the only times he's had homosexual intercourse—we're only talking a few times here, assuming you mean all-out intercourse—there was a condom involved, and never in any of those few occasions was that condom, um, *compromised*. So it's been a hundred percent on the safety side. My friend would still be able to give blood, right?"

Again, a headshake. "I'm afraid not. I'm not saying it makes total sense, but that's the law."

Now I was getting upset. Because this was the only thing I could do, and now I wasn't able to do it. For this crazy-ass bigoted reason.

"You mean to tell me, if my friend Amanda here had unprotected sex with a hundred guys and I had protected sex with two guys, she would be able to give blood and I wouldn't?"

People were definitely listening now. *Let them*, I thought.

"I'm afraid that's the law. Even if we don't agree with it, we can't let you give blood."

"*That's the law*. Of course that's the law! Because who would want to give a dying person *gay blood*. Even if it's screened for HIV and AIDS and everything else—no, if that person got some *gay blood*, who *knows* what might happen? Better to go without blood, right, than get it from a fag? That's a *great* law. It's, like, America's *best law ever*. I'm so fucking glad I live in this country!"

I guess I was lucky my shade of yellow wasn't any closer to brown, 'cause if I'd been Arab or easily mistaken for Arab, someone would've probably called the police. Don't get me wrong— there were plenty of people saying it wasn't fair, and there were even one or two leaving the line—whether because they'd had homosexual intercourse or because they sympathized with those of us who had, I don't know. I even felt sorry for the guy who was telling me all this, because clearly it wasn't his law, and clearly he had no desire to be having this conversation.

The line was moving forward, and we were just standing there.

"I'm sorry," the guy said.

I turned to Amanda. "Let's go. I know when I'm not wanted."

But Amanda wasn't moving.

"I can meet you later," she said. "I'll ask 'em to take double, so I can give for both of us."

That's not the point, I wanted to say, but I honestly wasn't clear what the point was anymore.

"Fine," I said. "I'll see you later." Even though I was pretty sure that I wouldn't. Amanda would spend the next couple of weeks calling, but I wasn't going to pick up.

I left the line and didn't look back. The air was as tainted as ever—it wasn't the kind of smell you got used to, the kind that your nose or your mind adjusts to. I checked my cell phone, and now it wasn't getting reception. I knew there were people around—even if my friends were off at school, many of their moms would have taken me in. But I didn't want to see any of them. So I just walked around for a while, seeing all the aimless people, picking up papers as I went—some of them the pages that had been pushed across the Hudson, some of them our own Brooklyn garbage, left behind for no reason other than there was no reason to keep them. Coupon sections from Sunday papers. Those Chinese take-out menus. Law firm receipts. Printed-out emails. Take-out menus from the World Trade Center area.

At one point I found myself walking by the entrance to the park, seeing all the people there, and I thought, *It can't be Tuesday.* It was unreal that it was a Tuesday and everybody was walking around. I could see the people who must've walked across the bridge, who were coming back from Manhattan looking exhausted, like it was night. You could tell that a lot of them had bonded in their journeys, and you really didn't know whether it was because they all worked in the same office or if they had just met as they forged across. I was seeing a lot of goodbyes—then hellos as people headed up their steps and made it to their own front doors. More often than not, there was someone waiting there to meet them, hold them, bring them inside.

I went back to my house. I sat down and turned on the TV and didn't get up for another six or seven hours. I flipped from newscast to newscast—they were all saying the same thing, and I guess it all depended on who you wanted to be telling it to you. I decided I wanted to be with Peter Jennings the most, because there was something about his accent that calmed me down. He made me know he was going through it along with me, that he was trying to figure out how to deal with what he had to do, too. They kept showing the same footage of the planes hitting the towers—then the fires at the Pentagon and the field in Pennsylvania, and everyone wondering if there were more targets, if more things were going to happen. At one point they'd repeated everything enough, and I wanted to tell them to stop showing the planes hitting the tower. We didn't need to see it again. And yet I didn't turn it off. Because I was hanging on every minute, wanting to be there when whatever was going to happen next actually happened. I tried flipping to other channels—the Food Network and Nickelodeon and VH1 Classic. But these channels felt like they were being beamed in from another planet, or even from the past—like the airwaves were taking a little longer to get here, so we could live in yesterday a little while longer, even if it felt wrong.

Around dinnertime, the phone rang again. I picked up and heard Mom's voice. She was just checking in, she said. She'd been trying for over an hour to get through.

"Isn't it early in the morning there?" I asked her.

And she said, "Do you really think I can sleep?"

There wasn't much I could tell her—she was watching the same news I was. And I wasn't going to tell her about giving blood—there was no reason to do that. I wasn't even sure she would take my side. If anything, she'd think I was using a roundabout way to tell her I had AIDS.

It wasn't like they were using the blood. They kept collecting it and collecting it for survivors who weren't being found. Maybe that's why I kept watching, and why Peter Jennings kept talking, and why I'm sure the streets of Brooklyn that night were lit by the blue flickerglow of all of our TV screens—because what we needed was that one moment of good news, that one person pulled from the rubble. I remembered how, when I was little, there was a baby girl who fell in a well, and it was like the whole country held its breath until they got her out. It's not that survivors would have erased what had happened to everyone else, but it would have at least told us that our hope was justified, that it was still the kind of story we were used to.

Instead the only victories we had were the things that hadn't happened. The fourth plane hadn't made it to D.C. There weren't fifty thousand people in the World Trade Center at 8:46 in the morning like there would've been at noon.

Darkness came, and I had to turn on the lights. The TV became too repetitive, and I had to put it on mute. My phone started working, and I had all these messages. And the whole time, all I could think about was how I'd really wanted to give blood and they hadn't let me.

I took a pizza out of the freezer and preheated the oven. I got a call through to my best friend in St. Louis but we only talked a little while. I unmuted the news and listened to it enough to know that nothing had changed since the last time I'd checked. I ate my pizza. I didn't pick up when I saw Amanda's number. I tried to watch a movie and couldn't.

I washed my dishes and put them on the rack to dry. Then I went back to my computer to tell more people I wasn't dead.

LOVE AND THEFT
Peter

The songs are wrong. The songs are wrong. This is what hits me: The songs are wrong.

I am at Tower Records, waiting to buy the new Bob Dylan, *Love and Theft*. I have Ryan Adams in my ears, but I turn the music off when the guy from Tower sees me outside, comes over early to unlock the doors, and says, "Man, do you know what's going on?"

It's the way he looks so sorry for me that makes me feel like I'm about to lose something. I can only stare at the blue dragon tattoo on his forearm and shake my head, not knowing until he tells me the news. I think for a moment it's a joke. And then I think, no, it isn't a joke.

I keep the music off, walk to Washington Square Park, look downtown—and there it is. I see it clearly. I'm standing there with strangers, and we're all talking as we stare at this dark, jagged hole in the right-hand tower. It looks, we all say, like a special effect from a big-budget science-fiction movie. This is our first way of grasping it. We are still in disbelief. More people come up and stop in shock. In the shadow of the crater you can see the fire. It seems so small to us—it isn't until we think about it that we realize the mark of flame is stories high. And the crater is the size of any of the buildings around us. The smoke has just started.

I know immediately that this is going to be one of the true historic moments of my life—that the personal and the historic are converging. I know people will ask, *Where were you when you first heard?*

Someone has a radio. We ask her our questions. *Did the plane go through the other side? What kind of plane was it? Are people getting out?*

I am not thinking in terms of people. I am thinking in terms of the building.

We say, *It's amazing it's still standing.* We say, *I can't believe this.* None of us—the ones watching from the park—seem to know anyone who works there. And we're sure we have to know someone who works there. New York isn't that big.

And then.

The middle of the second building shoots out in flames. We gasp. We cover our mouths. Some of us cry out.

There is a minute there, maybe less, where I stare at the Twin Towers and think there is some way that the fire has jumped from one building to the other—that it actually shot through the air and spread to the other tower. It makes no sense. But of course, I don't want it to make sense.

Then someone says he saw another plane. He says he'd noticed it, was wondering why it was flying so low. And that's when we cross over from disbelief into unbelief.

The second fire is stronger. Debris is falling. It looks like sheets of paper falling. But they are big. Too big. We know. *How many minutes was it between explosions? People could have evacuated, right? How can you fight a fire like that? Isn't it incredible that the buildings are still standing?* Horror on top of horror. Realizing each row of each tower is a floor. Each slit is a window. That there is nothing anyone can do. Sirens. We can hear sirens. I know I should be going to school. But I can't move. I cannot think of a single word to describe what we feel. I think we all feel it, to varying degrees. Perhaps in some other language there is a word for *the world is terribly wrong.* That feeling of stun and unbelief and abandonment and shock and horror and distress.

When the first tower collapses on itself, I feel it taking something away from us. And I'm sure it's something we won't get back again, at least not for a while. Maybe this is the moment that our unbelief turns slightly to belief.

Even as I start walking to school, I can't press play, because suddenly the songs are wrong—there's no music anymore, just news. Like when I would go on car rides with my parents, and as soon as I fell asleep, they'd pop the CD out and the car would be full of the news, repeating every half hour, only now it's like it's repeating every half second, and to hear anything else would be wrong. So my headphones stay around my throat as I stumble away. I know if I press play, the song will never be able to work for me again, because instead of the song playing under the moment, the moment will weigh on top of the song, and I am never going to want to remember this, I am never going to want to be here again, so I walk without anyone else's words in my ears, and all the music falls away from the world, because how can you have music on a day like today? White noise is not the same as silence. White noise is different because you know white noise is deliberate, composed to cancel everything out. It is the opposite of music, and it is all that I can hear and all that I can imagine hearing right now. I keep going back to that first moment— seeing the black hole on the tower, seeing the site of the crash. That image, that one image, is what I am picturing right now. That tower is our history, our lives, all the minutiae and security and hope. And that black hole is what I'm feeling. It is what has happened. It will affect me in ways I can't even begin to get my mind around. This day is a dark crater. There is no room for songs. The songs are wrong. Every song is wrong. And I don't know what to do without music.

THE NEXT HOURS AND THE NEXT DAYS

(Part Two)

THE DATE
Peter

After two days of being at home and not having school and not being able to go anywhere, I'm ready to leave the apartment. I tell my parents I'm going to stay over at John's house, because that's easier than the truth, and John's told me if it doesn't work out with Jasper717, then I can always show up late at night at his place, because his parents will assume it's Nicole sneaking in. John calls him Jasper717 because that's his email name, but I call him Jasper, and I'm really excited to see him, even though Mitchell's party seems like it was a long time ago, not this past Saturday. I'm nervous because I'm doing a lot of things I never do, such as (a) lying to my parents, (b) having a date with a boy who's in college, (c) leaving Manhattan, (d) wearing a deliberately tight T-shirt. This last one, (d), is because that's what I wore to Mitchell's party, and the first thing that Jasper said to me was, "Hey, that's a pretty tight T-shirt"—and at first I was all embarrassed, and then he said, "No, that's a good thing." The only people who flirt with me are usually the people who flirt with everyone, so I just thought, oh, he's playing a game. But every time he'd leave me for something—to get a drink, to talk

43

to someone else—he'd always loop his way back. When I went to Mitchell and asked who he was, Mitchell said, "Good—he asked who you were about fifteen minutes ago, and I've been waiting for you to catch up." I thought maybe it was my lucky night for once, because he seemed really nice, or at least like he knew what he was doing. Even when people started to leave, we kept talking—he was trying to tell me to apply to his school, and kept saying he'd love to host me for a visit, and I still wasn't convinced that he was really interested in me, and then he sat on my lap, which is about as unambiguous as it gets (other than actual sexual contact). I started to wonder if something was going to happen that very night, but when it got to be two in the morning, John and Veronica said they had to go, and Jasper said he was from Brooklyn, and I didn't know where he was staying, but I couldn't really ask him to stay at my place (because of my parents), and it didn't feel right trying to stay later at Mitchell's, because he'd started to gather all the bottles and glasses, which is a pretty obvious sign for everyone to go home and go to sleep. So I shrugged and said I had to go, and Jasper told me he was Jasper717 and even wrote it down so I'd have it, and I asked him if he'd seen *Hedwig*, and he said he hadn't, so we made a date, even if we didn't use the actual term *date*. I spent all of Monday worried and excited about it, and then Tuesday happened, and instantly the world was all out of whack, and I couldn't help being concerned about him, because all of a sudden he wasn't just this guy I'd met, he was the guy I was supposed to go out with on September 11th, and I felt that had to mean something. So we emailed a couple of times, and when the subways were mostly working again, we rescheduled for tonight, only instead of *Hedwig* he suggested I come over and watch a video, because his parents were stuck in Korea and not getting home anytime soon. I think this means something, too—not that his parents are in Korea, but that he's inviting me over. That seems more personal than a movie. So that's how I end up lying to my parents and telling John the truth, and then when the time comes, I take the F train out to Park Slope for this date that might not really be a date. When I get there, he meets me at the door and suggests a restaurant nearby. I say sure, because it isn't like I know anyplace else in the neighborhood. It's awkward at first, because even though we have this big thing in common—this September 11th connection—we still don't know each other that well. Even before we order, he asks me where I was when the planes hit, and I ask him where he was, and we compare notes. He's the first person I've known who missed it, who slept through it, and part of me is jealous that he didn't have to see it, and part of me is glad that I saw it, because otherwise it would be harder to believe. I feel I can tell him this, because it's not like it is with my parents, who are so worried about me being worried and who are so sad when they think I'm sad. He doesn't have to be affected by how it's affecting me, and that allows me to be honest. He's such a good listener that I don't even realize he's listening—I've been on dates before where the other guy makes it really obvious he's listening, and that's not really being a good listener, because that's asking to be noticed. But Jasper lets me talk, and when I say I'm babbling, he assures me I'm not. I think we're both a little shell-shocked from the week—there still aren't words to really explain it. I tell him how I've only just started listening to my disc player again, and even then I've had to pick my music really carefully. I have to read tracklists before I play a mix, which is something I never usually do, but now you never know what song's going to come on and bring it all back again. Like the new U2 album suddenly has this depth that it didn't have last week, because now when he sings "Walk On," he's singing to all of us. And Peter Gabriel's "Red Rain" appeared on a mix Dan had given me, and I almost lost it. Then I put on the mix Annie made me for my birthday, and this Amy Correia song, "Life Is Beautiful," came on, and she was singing about lying in the gutter and looking at the stars, and I thought, okay, there's still a lot of beauty in the world, even if I'm not feeling any of it. I tell Jasper about how the strangest things are making me cry, like this news story about these Starbucks employees who are staying up all night to stay open for hospital workers and rescue workers, and I ask him if he's had moments like that, too, crying at silly things, and he says he tends to detach from it all. "So you just withdraw?" I ask, not really knowing how someone could detach right now. And he says, "Not totally." Then, probably seeing I need more explanation, he adds, "I mean, you can't let it get to you." I say, "Because if you let it get to you, then the terrorists will have won?" This is a joke on my part, because for the past two days everyone's been saying things like, "You can't let the fear prevent you from drinking Coca-Cola . . . or the terrorists will have won" or "You can't put off buying that new Chevrolet . . . or the terrorists will have won." But Jasper doesn't seem to get my reference, or maybe he just doesn't know me enough to know I'm joking. Because he says, "It's not about them, really. It's just about me." I ask him when his parents are coming back, and he says they're trying, but they're not really sure. "When you stop all the airplanes in America, it tends to cause logistical problems." We talk about the news, and how much of it we've been watching, and I'm trying to sense whether or not the spark is there, the one that shot through us at Mitchell's party. Because even if it is there, I have to imagine it's been dulled by all the other things on our minds. One person on the news was saying they were already predicting a slew of "9/11 babies" nine months from now, but I wanted to say back to her, do you really think this is putting people in the mood? Not just for sex, but to have children? And I start to laugh, and Jasper asks me what I'm laughing at, and I say, "If we stop having sex, then the terrorists will have won." And I think, wow, he must think I'm a lunatic, but this time he actually laughs, too. I want to switch the subject before it takes us over again, so I ask him about college, but of course the answer he gives is that nobody knows if school's going to start on time this year, because people are afraid it's going to be hard to get there. And if . . . well, if there's another attack, people want to be home. "Do you really think there's going to be another attack?" I ask, and he says, "I don't know. But I think that's the whole point of it—that we have no idea." This is already the strangest date I've ever had,

47

because it's like *mortality* is factoring into it. And I can't even tell whether he's liking me, or whether we're just two people who happen to be sharing the same space for a certain amount of time. The restaurant is crowded, I think because most people are tired of being in their apartments, watching TV. There are even some groups of people who look like they're talking about other things, laughing and shouting over each other and debating. I ask Jasper what he's studying, and he tells me he's undecided—there isn't one thing that he gravitates toward. "I wish I could concentrate in General Studies," he says. "A little bit of this, a little bit of that." I nod, as if I've given the matter much thought. In truth, getting through senior year is intimidating enough. Even though I've only had four days of it, the pressure has been insane. But I don't tell him this, because I don't want to emphasize that I'm younger. I like it when he looks at me as an equal. It makes me believe I could be an equal, someday. "Have you ever seen *Cabaret*?" he asks, and I wonder if it's a trick question. I shake my head. "I mean, not the Broadway one, but the movie." I shake my head again. "Well, it's not *Hedwig,* but do you want to come back and watch *Cabaret* or something?" "Hells yes," I say, perhaps a little too eagerly. He smiles. "Looks like we have a plan, then." We split the check when it comes, then head outside. A gust of wind hits us, and I shudder. I wonder aloud when it's going to stop smelling like death, and Jasper says that, once again, he has no idea. But he says the waves of it are farther apart now—maybe that means it'll eventually wear itself out. His brownstone is only a couple of blocks away. It is not normal for me to go home with someone on a first date, but this feels like more than just a first date, and since Jasper's friends with Mitchell, it's not like he's a stranger. When we step inside the living room, it's a complete frat-house mess. Pizza boxes lie open-mouthed with congealed leftovers and petrified crusts still inside them. There's a forest of Snapple bottles settled with tea sediment, and a gaggle of magazines left haphazardly across the furniture—even though there's a couch and two armchairs, at first there's nowhere for me to sit. "Sorry, sorry," Jasper says, jumping in and clearing off the couch by moving everything into a makeshift pile on one of the armchairs. "I never did get that housekeeping merit badge." "You were a Boy Scout?" I ask. He nods. "An Eagle, actually. But without the housekeeping badge." He asks me if I want something to drink, and I tell him water would be great. And then he says, "No, I mean something to *drink*," and I say I'll have whatever he's having. He goes to the kitchen and brings back two bottles of OB beer. "OB?" I ask. And he says, "It's like Korean Budweiser. That way, if my parents catch me drunk, at least they'll think I'm reaffirming my heritage." Jasper turns on the TV, and of course it's the news, and all of a sudden we're sitting on the couch watching it, sipping our beers. Or at least I'm sipping; Jasper gulps. "Did you see Peter Jennings by the end of the day yesterday?" he says. "I swear, the man was up for forty-eight hours straight, trying to explain this unexplainable thing. If it weren't for him and Brokaw and Dan Rather, I think we would've had riots in the streets. They're the ones who calm us down. Not our fake of a president." "I'll drink to that," I say. He raises his beer. "To Peter Jennings!" "To Peter Jennings!" And then we clank our bottles, and I wonder whether this is the most contact we'll have tonight, because we go back to watching the news and all the talk about the Taliban and Osama bin Laden and what America's response should be. It's not very romantic, except maybe if you take the long view and say that the two of us on the couch despite everything going on is itself a romantic statement. *If we don't go out on dates, then the terrorists will have won.* After about an hour of CNN and ABC and NBC and CBS, with us providing our own commentary, Jasper (by now finishing his third beer, with me slowly imbibing my second) slaps his hand to his forehead and says, "*Cabaret!*" He digs up the DVD and puts it into the DVD player. "Is it okay if we leave the lights on?" he asks. "Or do you like it better in the dark?" And I say either way is fine. Truth is, I'm not really that interested in watching a movie. It's getting late, and my mind is slipping into its usual Clash refrain: Stay? Go? The movie starts, and Liza Minnelli's in pre-Nazi Germany, and it's a little weird because everyone seems to think she's amazing, but really she's not that attractive, but I'm afraid of saying anything, because for all I know, Liza Minnelli is Jasper's favorite actress ever, and even though I'm pretty new at this, I know that coming between a gay boy and his diva is a very serious offense. I personally don't have a diva, unless Rufus Wainwright and Morrissey count, which maybe they do. It's starting to feel like I'm over at a friend's house, which isn't a bad thing for a seventh date, but is pretty discouraging for a first. But there's no way I'm going to make a move without him giving me some indication that he wants me to make a move—which I guess is a way of me saying that he has to make the move, since indications are, in general, also moves. I try to motivate myself to take that first step, but the fact that it's his house and the fact that he's older and the fact that he's clearly more experienced than I am—well, it all just shuts me up, until I find a dull and neutral fact to send in his direction, to see what kind of response it gets. "It's almost midnight," I say after the British bisexual has stopped singing. And Jasper says, "You can stay over, you know. I mean, or you can leave. I don't want you to think you can't leave." "But I can stay." "Of course. It would be stupid to head all the way back to the Upper West Side at this hour. Unless, of course, you're going to get into trouble. . . ." "No—my parents think I'm at a friend's." He raises an eyebrow. "You little schemer, you." Sadly, my scheme doesn't include what to do next. "Do you want to watch the rest of the movie?" he asks. And I say yes, because I think it would be rude to say no. So we watch, and the Nazis ruin everything, and I'm starting to get really depressed. I'm surprised by a noise that's not coming from the screen, and then I realize—it's raining out. For the first time all week, it's raining. Then the movie's over, and when he hits stop, the news comes back on, and while they're not saying anything new—it's just new people analyzing—we still watch. Then Jasper starts to yawn, and when he yawns, I yawn, too. He smiles at that, but it's not an I'm-going-to-kiss-you-now smile. "We should probably go to bed," he says. Then he leaves the room. I fix my hair a little when he's gone, but when he comes back, he has sheets in his hand. "For the sofa," he explains. "Don't worry—it's really comfortable." And now I'm wondering why I didn't go home, if I'm only going to sleep on the lime-green couch. But now it's way too late to go home—or even to John's. So while Jasper brushes his teeth, I put the sheets on the couch. He offers me a toothbrush, and I go into the bathroom when he's done and look at myself in the mirror for a good long time, as if the reflection's going to tell me what to do. But instead of coming up with the answer, I stay in the land of inertia, which I guess is the same as deciding to accept defeat. It is, after all, just a first date. When I emerge from the bathroom, he's changed into an old white T-shirt and some boxers. This is unfairly sexy. He walks over and puts his arms around me and gives me a hug. "Sleep tight," he says. "I'm just down the hall if you need me." And of course in this situation, none of the questions I want to ask—"Don't you like me?" "Am I that unattractive to you?" "Can't I join you?"—are appropriate. So I go to the couch and lie down and clutch at the cushions. It's ridiculous to think I'll be able to go to sleep, so I turn the TV back on. Then I'm worried it's too loud, so I put it one notch above mute and keep it on CNN, so even if I can't hear what they're saying, I can use the crawling text at the bottom to read myself to sleep. A half hour passes, and the storm outside is getting stronger—there's even thunder now, and that sound of raindrops hitting branches and pavement. I hear a door open, and then Jasper is back in the room. He comes right over and sits down on me, right on my legs, like I'm part of the couch. "Hello," he says. And I say,

"Hello." Then he asks, "What are you doing?" And I'm thinking, *I'm trying to sleep on the couch*, but I don't say that. He bounces up and down on me a little, like a kid. "Isn't the couch comfy?" he says. I can only say, "I guess." "But why are you sleeping here?" he asks. And I honestly think that's not a question I should have to answer. He bounces on me again, then stands up and offers his hand. "Come on." So I take his hand, and he pulls me up off the couch, and we leave the TV on as we walk to his room. The bed's the only part of the room that's cleared off, and I assume we're going to end up there. First, though, we stop at the window, because he's left it open, and there's lightning now as well as thunder, and the rain is coming down hard. "Look at that," he says, and while I do look at that, I'm also looking at him, and in this gray-tone light, he couldn't be more attractive. In the shadow of that window, right at that moment, we are both luminous. He's let go of my hand, and I try to take his back, but he just smiles. "Aren't you going to kiss me?" he asks. So I lean in and kiss him, but it's not as warm as I thought it would be. When I pull back, he's still observing. "Is that all?" he asks. It's cold in the room, from the window, an end-of-summer chill. And I stand there, waiting. Because I do want to kiss him, and I do want to sleep in that bed, but when I kiss him again, it's the same feeling of incompleteness, and I don't know what to do with that. "What's going on?" I ask. And he says, "I guess it's raining." And I say, "That's not what I meant." Which only causes him to say, "I'm sorry. This was a bad idea. I should have left you alone." Finally I decide to take a stand, and I say, "I'll just

53

go back to the couch." And he says, "No, you can stay here. We can just sleep." But there's no way I'm going to be able to sleep next to him like it isn't weird—there's no way I want to stay if staying means nothing. I already feel such a deep sense of being lost—something even more fundamental than confusion, the dark equivalent of white noise. So I say I'll go back to the couch, and he pulls me into a hug again, and we stay like that for a little while, to the point that it's almost like we're slow dancing. We just sway on the same spot as time beats out an empty tune. I look out the window, and the sky lights up into a pure view of electricity. Then he lets me go, and I go. I head back to the couch, turn off the news, and try to sleep. In the morning, he offers me breakfast, and I say I really need to get back home. I have my disappointment and confusion, and he has whatever it is that he has. He acts like nothing happened, and I act like nothing happened. We both hold on to that delicate lie.

LIMBO
Jasper

I felt there was a piece of me missing, a piece that had become so unnerved that it fell away without me feeling it. I didn't even know what piece it was—I just felt the gap, and knew that whatever it was, it must have been important.

I didn't really leave the house. This wasn't all that different from my original plan for when Mom and Dad were gone, only now there were people calling all the time, checking to see how I was, asking me if I wanted to meet up. It was like some mass email had gone out, and everybody was going out of their way to prove to me that we still lived in a caring universe. But I didn't want any of it. The good thing about everyone's post-disaster catatonia was that nobody wanted to be intrusive—they'd express concern or issue an invitation, but they were more than understanding if you said, "I just want to be alone right now." So that's what I did. I didn't rant like a crazy person. I didn't tell them to fuck off. I didn't ask them what the point was. I just said I wanted to be alone. And then when I was alone, I ranted like a crazy person, told the world to fuck off, and wondered what the point was.

The only exception I made was this boy Peter, because he

was so persistent it was almost surreal. He made it seem like us getting together was a belief he had. So finally I told myself what the hell. I made him come out to Brooklyn, because there was no way I was going into Manhattan until it had straightened itself out. My initial impulse to go save it was gone. The more footage they showed on the news, the more horror stories we heard, the less I wanted to be there. I would just stay in Brooklyn and listen to my *Moulin Rouge* soundtrack on repeat until the happy times were here again. Or until I had to go to school—whichever came first.

Mom was calling two or three times a day—it was probably costing them more than their plane tickets to keep in touch. She wanted to come home as soon as possible, but I kept telling her I was fine, that she and my father should stick to the original plan and take care of my grandmother and let all the other people who were stranded in Korea get home first.

It was a testament to my respect for Peter that I actually found a clean shirt and a relatively clean pair of jeans to wear for our night out. The truth was, I wasn't remembering much of what he looked like or what we'd talked about at Mitchell's. I remembered thinking he was cute, if a little young. But that was enough. I also sensed that he was as trapped in his house as I was trapped in mine, because I would get emails from him like

jasper—

only 8 more hours! i will be the guy in the brown tshirt and the levis. also, i will be the

one ringing your doorbell. if that is not
enough to recognize me, i could also have a
tulip between my teeth. or behind my ear, if
you would find that more aesthetically pleas-
ing. i have both a florist and a dresser on
standby, awaiting your answer.

see you soon (say, seven hours and fifty-five
minutes?)
peter

Seven hours and fifty-five minutes later, he was at my front door.
His T-shirt really fit him well, and he was boyish in a Ewan Mc-
Gregor kind of way, albeit without the brogue.

I took him to Olive Vine—I knew there was a chance of
bumping into some of the people I'd been dodging, but I figured
that would be a risk anywhere. It's not like anyone was leaving
the neighborhood. Flags were starting to pop up everywhere,
along with the MISSING signs. It was like we'd cleared away all
the papers that had blown over and were replacing them with
our own.

I was relieved, because clearly Peter wasn't a closet case,
and he seemed to know what some of the dating rules were. Not
that I was seeing it as a date—more as a diversion. It's not like I
was going to put him in my pocket and take him up to college
with me. And he didn't seem like the random-hookup type. (A
shame. Or maybe not.) I asked him all the things I felt I should
ask, like where he'd been when everything happened. He told
me he was waiting to buy a Bob Dylan record, which I thought

was pretty funny. "The times, they did a-change?" I said, but his laugh was more polite than anything else. I chalked it up to the fact that you had to be twisted like me to find the humor in the situation.

Usually I treated dates like they were chess matches, trying to plan my moves a little bit ahead, carefully deciding which conversational pieces to deploy, willing to sacrifice pawns of small talk if it would get my opponent to fall in love with my king. But this was a different kind of board, a different set of rules—almost like all the pieces had been knocked off, and we were both trying to agree on where they'd been before. I wasn't having any fun with it, which wasn't his fault. Fun was included in the piece of me that had disappeared.

He talked about seeing things happen, about being near, and while he expressed a momentary jealousy that I hadn't had to go through that, I think we both knew that it was better to be an unharmed witness than the guy who slept through it and still had to deal with the aftermath. One of the things the terrorist attack has done was to send us all into these *Sliding Doors* scenarios—all these what ifs. What if I'd gotten up earlier that morning? What if I'd decided to go to Battery Park for a run? I'd done that once . . . in 1998, before the SATs. What if, along the way, I'd taken the spot on a crowded subway car that some guy who worked at the World Trade Center was supposed to take, so the doors slid closed on him and he ended up getting to work late enough to be saved? Bullshit—all of it complete bullshit. And you couldn't help but wonder why your mind went there anyway—was it to exert control or to find comfort in the fact that there wasn't really all that much control, after all?

By the time I tuned back in, Peter was talking about crying because people at Starbucks were being extra nice. The fact that he could be so moved only reinforced my own emptiness. When he asked me how I felt, I didn't lie—it didn't seem like the kind of thing to lie about. And I found myself telling him—or at least trying to—about how the emptiness worked, how you withdraw from something and you feel the distance inside of you as well as outside of you. But it was clear he wasn't really understanding, and that made me wonder yet again why I'd agreed to meet up with him. Clearly, there wasn't much I could give him, and there wasn't much he could give me.

"So you just withdraw?" he asked me. And I couldn't convey to him the extent of it, so I just said, "Not totally." Then, since that didn't seem like enough, I added, "I mean, you can't let it get to you."

"Because if you let it get to you, then the terrorists will have won?"

I wished it were as simple as that. But it wasn't.

"It's not about them, really," I said. "It's just about me."

I knew how monstrous that sounded—I knew September 11th wasn't about me. But my reaction to September 11th—that was *entirely* about me.

Peter quickly switched the subject to my parents, and I gave him the update. I was totally running out of steam until he drifted off and then, when he came back, said, "If we stop having sex, then the terrorists will have won." Normally, when someone says something like that, it's a total bad pickup line, but it was obvious that wasn't Peter's intention, and I liked him more for it. He asked me about school, and I told him I had no idea when it was going to start—yet another thing I had no idea about. Like any high school student, he had this fascination with college, and I found myself getting nostalgic—if September 11th was really going to be this big before/after dividing line in our lives, I was sorry that I didn't have at least a bit of high school in the after. High school actually seemed longer ago now because of what had happened.

I tried to imagine Peter up at school with me. I tried to imagine us as boyfriends, and it felt about as realistic as me dating Sarah Jessica Parker. I knew what I had to do: get the check, say goodbye, send him on his way. But one of the missing parts of me made a slight guest appearance, because I also felt this strange *fondness* for him, like he was a stray and I had to take him home and give him a bowl of milk. That, and I didn't particularly love the idea of going back to the house again and spending another night in the company of the TV set. At least Peter wouldn't expect the same things from me that my parents or my friends would.

So I found myself asking him over, and he seemed up for it. It was a little weird at first, because having him in the living room made me realize what a shitheap it had become, like I'd let objects fall from my hands whenever I was done with them, my very own sculpture garden of a ruined week.

"Sorry, sorry," I said. I almost added, "The housekeeper is in mourning." But that was pretty awful, so I added, "I never did get that housekeeping merit badge."

"You were a Boy Scout?" he replied, totally interested. And I didn't have the heart to tell him that no, I wasn't—somehow the scouts filled their gay Korean Brooklynite quota without me. So I nodded, and I lied, and while I lied, I decided to make myself an Eagle Scout.

Hoping to make my way back to being a good host, I offered him a drink, and clarified what kind of drinks I was offering when he seemed to want water—which is acceptable if you've just run a few miles, but not really in a social situation. Since the local bodega owners would only laugh if I showed them my fake ID, I had to resort to my parents' stash of Korean beer, which was probably great if you'd never left Korea and had never tasted any other beers, but was pretty damn unexceptional if you'd ever kept the company of Mr. Samuel Adams and his brethren.

Peter sipped the OB politely and declined to make the usual OB-GYN jokes about its name. We watched the news for a while, and I pretty much confessed my crush on Peter Jennings. And maybe it was all the talk of Peter Jennings, but suddenly I was like, *Why am I here on the couch with this seventeen-year-old Ewanish boy and totally keeping my hands to myself? Was it him or was it me that was stopping us?* I figured he'd be into it, but I didn't want to freak him out if he wasn't. I decided to turn the flirtation up a notch, remembering that I'd said we were going to watch *Cabaret*. Once I put the movie on, I asked him if he liked the lights on or off—clearly code words for "Do you want to sit here like we've been sitting or do you want to start making out?" He said he could do either, which was no help whatsoever.

The movie started, and I wasn't remotely interested in it. I slid a little closer to him, but it was a completely missed signal. After a while I realized how late it was getting, and I wondered if Peter was planning on going home or staying over. Finally he pointed out that it was almost midnight, and it was really clear in his voice that he wanted to stay. I thought of him trying to get the subway all the way back, and I knew I couldn't do that to him. But I also didn't want him to think he *had* to stay, because I knew I was going to crash pretty soon. When I asked him if he was going to get in trouble with his parents, he told me he'd already made up an alibi for them. This got my attention—he was playing a little more of a game than I'd pegged him for. Still, he didn't make a move. I figured we could start making out during the rest of the DVD, so we restarted it, and I realized too late that even though it has music, *Cabaret* is a fucking downer of a movie, as most things that end with the Holocaust tend to be.

Soon Sally Bowles's party was over, and it looked like ours was going to follow suit. I could barely keep my eyes open, and every time I yawned, Peter would echo it with another yawn. I tried to feel some kind of sexual current in the room, but came up with more yawning. Maybe my receptors were out of commission. I told him it was probably time to call it a night. And I realized that there was no way we were going to sleep in the same bed—that would lead him on too much, and I didn't want to lead him on. The right thing to do was to leave him alone.

I could hear the rain outside, and I opened my window and breathed a little of it in before I got the sheets for the couch. I could've given him my parents' room, but I could imagine them making a late-night arrival at JFK, then cabbing home to find a complete boy-stranger in their bed. (It would be even worse if they found him in my bed . . . with me.) I knew I should have explained this to him, but I was too tired even for that. I figured he'd just go with it, and it would be fine.

But he looked disappointed when he saw the sheets, and even though I told him the sofa was really comfortable, I knew it wasn't the sleep that he was worried about. I felt like my blood was venom now, for ruining this kid's night like this, but I wasn't in the mood to be with anyone. At least not until I was back in my room with the door closed, trying to go to sleep. I'd made the mistake of hugging him good night, and it was odd how that stayed with me. It wasn't meant as anything but friendliness. But I started to imagine him in my bed, us just holding each other, and that started to sound good to me. Outside, it was all thunder and lightning—real spooky-movie stuff. I could hear him shuffling around in the living room, watching the TV on low, trying to fall asleep to the news that was keeping us all awake. I had no idea what I wanted, only that I wanted *something*, which is the worst kind of wanting. I sat up in bed and stayed like that for a good fifteen minutes. Finally I decided I'd just go and check on him, and when I did, I found him completely awake. There was no place on the couch to sit, so I just sat lightly on his legs.

"Hello," I said.

"Hello," he said.

Little simple words.

"Isn't the couch comfy?" I lifted myself a little so I wouldn't crush him, then eased back down.

"I guess," he mumbled.

I was still going back/forth, yes/no, leave/make out.

Finally I pushed it.

"But why are you sleeping here?" I asked, falling back on flirtation. When I didn't get a response—yes, he was a little miffed—I stood up, gave him my hand, and told him to come on. I was still searching for that current—or maybe I was trying to manufacture it. But even as we walked to my room, holding hands, I felt the voltage start to diminish. We veered toward the open window and stood there silent for a little while. Even on a regular night, hard rain like this would have made us notice. But now it seemed almost biblical in its appearance. Wash us clean, maybe. Or drown us all.

I'd let go of his hand without really meaning to. It's just hard to hold a hand for that long. But then he made this completely obvious move to take it back, and I thought he was finally going to push me into something. Instead he backed away.

I goaded him. "Aren't you going to kiss me?" A line I'd used before.

And it worked, because almost immediately he was leaning into me. And it didn't work, because the emptiness came back.

It made me angry. Mostly at myself. And also at him. For his stupid innocence. For making me think I could be woken up by a kiss.

I found myself saying, "Is that all?" Goading him again. Pushing him harder. Letting it be like that.

And he heard that. He kissed me again.

I wanted to feel something. But I couldn't get to it. Maybe with someone else, someone yet to be found. But not with him.

"What's going on?" he asked. Like I knew. Like any of us knew.

"I guess it's raining," I said, wanting him to find me on his own, because I couldn't find myself.

And I got that disappointment again.

"That's not what I meant," he said.

What did I feel? Something between sleepwalking and defeat. Something between victim and victimizer.

"I'm sorry," I said. "This was a bad idea. I should have left you alone."

This was not what he wanted to hear.

"I'll just go back to the couch," he said, already moving to leave.

"No," I said, trying to stop him. "You can stay here. We can just sleep."

Not sex. Just us next to each other.

But he couldn't see it. He insisted on returning to the

couch, and I felt he was giving me my own punishment, one I deserved. I tried to hold him—I tried one more hug, tried to get what I needed there—but it didn't last for long. The night was over. He stared out the window, and there was nothing to see— not Manhattan, just Brooklyn. Nobody working around the clock, nobody digging, nobody searching for a miracle. Just rain and lightning and darkness.

I could hear him after he left. Back on the couch, shifting from side to side. I stayed standing by the window. I had no idea what had just happened, and I knew he didn't, either. I had never felt so much like my life was not my own, that I was just a vessel for things I would never understand. I didn't want him . . . but if I didn't want him, what did I want? I didn't want to be alone . . . but if I didn't want to be alone, then why didn't I want to be with anyone else?

Limbo is the state where there are only questions.

That was as far as I'd gotten.

I CAN'T SLEEP
Claire

I can't sleep.

It's not just the sound of the rain outside. It's not the unfamiliarity of the bed I'm lying in. It's not my mother's deep, uneasy breathing next to me. It's the thoughts. They will not go to sleep, so I cannot go to sleep.

The bedroom we're sleeping in was once Rana's. Now it's a guest room. You can only find traces of her in the folds, the corners no one cares about. Even though this is our third night sleeping here, I'm still not used to it. Nor am I used to sharing a bed with my mother. I can't remember ever climbing into bed with her when I was a girl, not even after a nightmare or during a storm like this. She wasn't that kind of mother, and I wasn't that kind of daughter. I don't think we're about to start now. She looks older when she's asleep, and this alarms me. She looks like the act of sleep is exhausting her as much as the act of living.

I wanted to go back to our apartment, but we were told we couldn't. Three times, we walked down to the barricades on Canal Street and let the police officers know where we lived. Each time, they said it was still too dangerous. They asked us if

67

we had a place to stay. "We just want to see it," I said, even though I knew there was no point.

When I picture my room, I imagine everything covered in ashes. I know the windows are closed. I know the door is shut. But I imagine death as a fine dust that's gotten in through the cracks, that covers my unmade bed, my clothes, my carpet. In my mind, it looks like a hundred years have passed, draining away all the color. The air itself has decayed and fallen to the floor.

I try to think of other things, but there are no other things. This is the only thing I can think about.

Every time I've walked downtown—every time I've looked downtown—it's been the same. First the smoke. Then the source of the smoke. And the disappearance. How the other buildings, which once seemed so small in comparison, have now revealed their true height.

Gone. One of the words that's hardest to fully comprehend. *Gone.*

I feel the urge to weep, the kind of weeping that feels like you are choking on a thick black cloud. I manage to keep it in, but barely. Walking back here tonight, right before dinner, a woman passed me, and she was laughing. A dancing, happy laugh. I can still see her. She was walking downtown—she could see the smoke, if she looked. And she was laughing at something her companion had said. And I thought, *How can you?*

It is unbelievable to see the city so shut down. It is unbelievable that there are no planes in the sky. It is unbelievable that none of us know the full impact yet.

I could take the leather-bound *Little Women* off of Rana's bookshelf and read it in the bathroom, where the light won't disturb anyone. Or I could go into the den, where Sammy's asleep, and turn on the television, muted, looking for the one channel that will pretend nothing's happened. If only I still had my faith in old books and reruns. They are among the things I feel have been taken from me, along with humor and hope and the ability to savor. I could go into the kitchen and steal some ice cream from the freezer, but it would only taste like cold on my tongue. I could put on headphones and listen to a CD, but it would only sound like disturbed airwaves, not music. So I stay in bed until the thunder stops and Mom's sleep-breathing slows and my thoughts become so loud that I can't take it anymore. Because after the storm there's something even scarier outside—an astounding, uncitylike quiet. I don't hear any cars going by, no voices. There are no clocks ticking in the apartment, no gusts of wind pressing against the glass. It's as if the rain has washed all the life away, except for the water finding the openings in the pavement, seeping down.

I have to get out of here. Being here makes me remember that I'm not home. It makes me remember why I'm not home.

I set my feet quietly on the floor, careful not to take any of the sheets with me, trying to levitate from the mattress so Mom won't feel me shift. I have been sleeping in my clothes, and nobody has questioned this. Now that I'm up, I feel unwashed, but I worry that the simple act of turning on the faucet will wake up not just the sink and the pipes, but the whole apartment. So I change into new socks and carry my shoes into the den. I want Sammy to be up, so I can ask him to come with me. But when I look at the couch, I find him floating in a dream cloud. The least I can do is let him have that.

It's only when I get to the front door that I put on my shoes. I unlock the security bolts and take the spare key. This is new territory for me—I never sneak out. But this thing—this thing that's happening—has made me not care what I normally do. Sneaking out now doesn't have to mean that I'm used to it, or that I'll ever do it again. It's what this specific moment calls for.

I close the door and walk down the hallway, my steps as silent as the walls. No one is watching TV at this hour. No one is arguing. If there are sleepwalkers, they hide their presence the same way I do. Once I'm out the door, I realize I should have left a note. But it's too late. I need to keep going.

I don't have a watch on or a phone with me, so I don't know what time it is. *2:18, 3:12, 3:45, 4:06*—what's the difference, really? I walk outside and it's absolute night, not yet softened by the coming of the day. There is some reassurance in the fact that the streetlamps are still working and the air is, at least temporarily, less caustic as I inhale. I wonder if the storm has put out the fires at Ground Zero or if this is only a pause before the smoke from below reaches back into the sky. It is too dark and too distant for me to see if the plumes are still there. On Eighteenth Street you can't see much farther than Eighteenth Street. When a cab drives by, I'm almost grateful for the sign of life.

Crossing Third Avenue, I start to see people. Not many, but

a few. This is not a late-night crowd. These are not people coming home from bars or clubs. Nor are they workers coming home from a graveyard shift. I can tell: These are people like me. The relocated. They have not been sleeping in their own beds. They are wrecked by the devastating side effects of such helplessness, most notably insomnia. They might be tourists stranded in hotels. There are some, I have no doubt, who are still looking for the missing, still clutching the thinnest available hope. I don't make eye contact with them. I'm afraid of their stories. That's what it's been like lately—we have the ability to glimpse each other as souls. Damaged, frightened, confused, caring souls.

The posters—all those homemade posters—are sagging under the weight of the rain. The words bleed as the damp paper pulls against the Scotch tape. The posters around telephone poles have shaped themselves to the wood, the old staples showing through like scars. Others have fallen face-first onto the sidewalk, or have been carried into clogged gutters. Nobody was thinking of rain. Nobody would have waited the extra hour to make the posters waterproof. The words that remain intact are the biggest ones, the ones you'd most expect—MISSING and HAVE YOU SEEN ME? It's the photos and the phone numbers that have lost their focus. If you look at them with your naked eye, it's like you're seeing them through tears. They have the same kind of blur.

I was going to walk aimlessly, one direction as good as any other, but now I want to go to Union Square. If I can't go home,

I'll go there. Seeing the rain-ruined posters, I want to turn my wandering into a pilgrimage. I want to see the shrine. I want to go back to see all the candles and portraits and banners and notes. For the past three days, people have been going to Union Square to mourn and pray, leaving their remembrances alongside everyone else's. I have no idea who put the first candle down, which strangers first gathered and named it a gathering place. I went there on Wednesday morning because I saw other people were going there, and ever since, I haven't been able to come back to Ted and Lia's apartment without stopping there first. It's what I need. Even in the middle of the night, even (especially) when I'm alone. Every inch of it is heartbreaking, and that's what I want to do right now—I want to break my own heart.

"It's going to be all right," my mother keeps telling me. And I want to tell her what she says is impossible—there is no such thing as *all right*. The lie is in the word *all*.

There are more cars on the streets now—nothing so busy that you'd call it traffic. In fact, most of the cars are empty cabs, as trapped in the searching as we are. The people out right now don't want to take cabs. We just want to walk. Our legs need to move to keep our minds from collapsing.

I wish there was somebody I could call. I wish there was somebody who I could wake up at whatever time it is and say, "I need you to come to Union Square and be with me right this minute." But my best friends aren't that close—not in terms of distance to Union Square, and not in terms of closeness to me. They're friends I could call at six at night, but not at six in the morning. If I had a boyfriend, maybe I could call him. But I don't, so it's a stupid thing to think about.

Here's what breaks us: Even though we know better, we still want everything to be all right.

I think about Marisol and wonder how she and her sister are doing. I would never call her at six in the morning. I don't even know her last name.

I think about Jill Breslin and how her father is dead—the school sent out an email telling us, confirming it. What I'm feeling is nothing—*nothing*—compared to what she and her family are feeling. It makes me feel safer, but also smaller.

As I'm crossing Park Avenue, about to get to the square, another downpour hits. I didn't bring an umbrella, so I just let it batter me. I feel the sinking cold, and I can't help but wonder if there are ashes in the raindrops. I picture them there—a little filament of ash in each tiny upside-down bulb of water. I shiver.

There are a few people in ponchos on the square, and a few police officers. It's nothing like it is during the day—the crowded museum of sadness and pain is largely closed for the night, making us the night watchmen. There isn't an empty railing to be found; they all have wreaths and posters and photos of the missing, who we all know are dead. One piece of paper says TERRORISTS: WE WILL FIND YOU AND KILL YOU. But mostly people want to commemorate the lost. There are testimonials to the firefighters, the NYPD officers, the Port Authority police. There are flags, so many flags. There are kids' drawings on oak-tag paper, the Magic Marker smudging now, so the towers have become gray moats, the Statue of Liberty has melted into a puddle. So many people saying thank you, and it's all wet and ruined. Messages that will never be read. Gifts that were given too late.

The worst is the candles. They're all out. They stand there blankly, more crooked than upright. They were left to fend for themselves, carry their own vigil, and they failed. They're just sticks of wax. They have nothing.

Suddenly I'm crying. I can't stop crying. This is just too much. The enormity of it is crushing me. Because I am still foolish enough to have believed I would find something here that could help me, that I would wander out into the night and find something that would make me feel better. What a small, almost petty thing to want—to feel better.

I sit down on a bench, even though I don't feel I have any right to sit on a bench, here among the dead and the missing and the remembered. In small letters, someone has written NEVER FORGET on one of the slats. I know it's supposed to be a pledge, but it feels like a curse. Don't we have to forget some of it? Don't we have to forget this feeling? If we don't, how will we live?

I want to kneel down to every photograph. I want to stop the ground from turning to mud. I want the rain to dissolve me instead of the notes that people have left on the grass. I want one person—just one single person—who is missing to still be alive.

Breathing is hard. When you cry so much, it makes you realize that breathing is hard.

People walk past me. They leave me to myself, which is different from leaving me alone.

I look over to the south side of the square and see this one woman lighting a candle. She cups her hand over it, even though the rain is now just a drizzle. She leans in with a lighter until the wick takes hold of the flame. Leaving her hand there for a second, sheltering it. Then moving her hand away.

She's wearing a raincoat—a formless green raincoat—and it's still darkish out, so it's hard for me to tell anything about her, except that she has long, dark hair. She looks once at the candle and the framed photo behind it, then moves on to the next candle. Again, she cups her hand. Again, she flicks her lighter. Again, she waits for the flame to catch.

I watch her for a minute. It's like we're the only two people in the park, and I am afraid that even by watching, I am disturbing her. But then she lights a third candle, and a fourth, and my crying has stopped, and I feel foolish again. But at least it's the kind of foolish that will get me to do something.

I stand up from the bench and smooth out my shirt. I walk over and get within ten feet of the woman before I hesitate again. She is so intent on the candles that I'm afraid I will startle her. I look back at her work—the second candle she lit is out again, but the rest are still flickering.

"Excuse me," I say.

She looks surprised. While I've been watching her, she hasn't noticed me at all.

"Can I help you?" I ask.

She is not expecting this. I see now she's about my mother's age, and her hair is wet enough to make me think she's been doing this for a while now. All through the night, even.

"I only have one lighter," she says apologetically.

"I could use that," I say, pointing to the candle she's just lit.

"Here." She reaches over and picks it up. We both look at the photo it was sitting in front of, a man in his fifties. There's no MISSING or HAVE YOU SEEN ME? or even a name. It's just a framed photo that somebody left. I can easily imagine it sitting on a mantelpiece or on a desk. Or on top of a casket at a funeral. There are going to be so many funerals at once.

"I don't think he'll mind," the woman says gently, nodding at the man in the photograph. She reaches the candle over to me, and I take it from her. For a moment, both our hands are on it. She's watching the flame, willing it to stay alight.

"Thank you," I say.

"It's nothing," she tells me. "Thank *you*."

This, I think, is how people survive: Even when horrible things have been done to us, we can still find gratitude in one another.

I decide to go back to the first candle she lit and move in the opposite direction around the path. Before I do, I look back and observe again how she does it. When she pauses before each one, I look to see if her lips move, if she's actually saying a prayer. But whatever words she's thinking are kept to herself, or sent directly to whoever she believes can hear her thoughts, deity or deceased.

I can't think of anything to say. I don't know these people whose candles I am lighting. So instead, as I light each one, I am sure to read the names out loud, if there are names. I am sure to look each photo in the eye, if there's a photo. I cup my hand over each unlit candle, then raise my own candle to it. They touch, and I leave a small flame. Sometimes it doesn't last, or it doesn't work at all. Sometimes I have to wipe off the water that's pooled in the hollow of the wax. Sometimes I have to backtrack when my candle goes out, and relight it on one of the candles I lit only moments before. Every now and then I look to see how the woman in the green raincoat is doing. Two other people, a couple, have seen us and are now using their own lighter to save more candles. It feels like the right thing to do, even though the light we make doesn't change what's happened. We are making our own temporary constellation, and it doesn't spell a single thing.

I keep going. The rain returns and becomes more insistent. I guard my candle, and when it runs too low, I borrow another one. I don't try to relight the ones I've lit that have gone out again. I just keep going. At certain points I'm aware people are watching, but then I go back to reciting the names, lighting the candles. There are so many of them. I have to keep going. What separates us from the animals, what separates us from the chaos, is our ability to mourn people we've never met. I light candle after candle after candle.

It's pointless, but it's the only thing I can do.

THE DROWN OF THINGS AND THE SWIM OF THINGS

(Part Three)

TURN
Peter

I'm brought back to life by Travis. Not a guy named Travis. No—the band Travis. Musically, they may be a blip on the Brit-pop radar—but in September 2001, they are big enough to sell out Radio City Music Hall. The only question is: Will the concert actually happen?

It's not looking good. In the week after 9/11, New York City becomes something it hasn't been since the days before the steamship: isolated. Even after the bridges and tunnels and airports open again, most of the people who are using them are making a return voyage. The tourists disappear. Bands do not show up. Concerts are canceled left and right. Museums are empty. New York is full of . . . New Yorkers.

Nobody knows what will happen.

School starts again on Monday, six days after. It starts with an assembly and a minute of silence for Jill Breslin's dad and all the others who lost their lives. Then we're told that we need to try to go back to normal, or as close to normal as we can get. Classes will resume. Activities will resume. Life will resume for the living. Counselors are available if we have problems with that.

Because I wasn't here when it happened—because I was skipping study hall to stand outside Tower Records and didn't show up until after everything had been destroyed—I wondered if it would be weird, like there was something I wasn't going to share with everyone else. But now I see that's not true. Because I did see most of my classmates that day. And even the ones I didn't, we were all here, we were all a part of it. And suddenly I'm feeling this—I guess you could call it tenderness—for people I never even liked before. It's yet another unexpected aftershock—that I can look at Carly Fisher chewing her gum, rolling her eyes, and even though I have never been able to muster up anything more than annoyance when it comes to her, suddenly there's this base level of caring. And the people I care about, suddenly I care about them a little more, in this existential way. Like my best friend, John, who actually went to Tower on the twelfth and bought me a copy of *Love and Theft* instead of just burning me a copy of the one he bought for himself. Or Claire, who is telling everyone they should go out and volunteer—not for one of the 9/11 charities, but for all the other charities that are going to be hit hard because everyone's going to give to the 9/11 charities now. Or Aiden, the first boy I kissed, who probably went clubbing this weekend and managed to forget everything that happened, if only for the length of a song. I am full of this wide gladness that they're all okay. Flawed and miserable and sleepless. But alive.

It doesn't feel like normal, though. It's not just caring that's been added—there's also fear. Every time there's a siren in the street. Every time the PA coughs to life, even if it ends up being the announcement of a food drive. Every time we remember, which is constant.

At lunch, John asks me how the date with Jasper717 went, and I tell him I can't even begin to explain it. It feels like it was all some kind of twisted dream, the kind where your bedroom door leads to Paris and your mother doesn't remember you're her son, so she insists that you have to run a marathon underwater.

"Sounds like fun," John says.

"Like kissing a steamroller," I tell him.

I'm still—I don't know—impressed that John asks me about my dates and everything, because he's straight and he doesn't really have to. I never thought I'd lose his friendship over the whole gay thing, but I also didn't think he'd be very interested.

I tell him I did get an email from Jasper717 the next day, apologizing for being so scattered, for "sending mixed signals." But he didn't offer to make it up to me, and I was glad.

"So that's that," John says.

"Exactly."

We switch back to talking about music, and how the rumors are true that the CMJ Festival has been canceled and that most acts are pulling out of shows for the next few weeks. It's too hard to get here. Or maybe they're just scared. I can't say I blame them. Even though we New Yorkers have been hitting the streets and the stores and the restaurants, I can't say any of us has had much desire to go to the top of the Empire State Building or spend much time in Times Square or gather by the tens of thousands in Madison Square Garden. In other words, we feel like if we stick to the quieter places, we won't be targets. It's a hard thing to get over.

"Think Travis will cancel?" John asks me. We're supposed to go together.

"Probably," I say. "I mean, wouldn't you?"

John shakes his head. "No, I would not. I would play, man."

And I think, of course he would. And I wonder why I thought I wouldn't.

We check the website. We call the theater. We listen to updates on the radio. The day comes, and the concert hasn't been canceled. The band has made it to town.

I meet up with John that night and I'm nervous about going to midtown. Which is insane—it's pretty ridiculous to imagine Osama bin Laden in a cave in Afghanistan telling his minions, "We got the World Trade Center, we got the Pentagon, we missed the White House, but now we're going to get . . . Travis!" But I guess the thing about fear is that it defies the laws of rationality. It creates its own laws instead.

"What's wrong?" John asks as we get close to Radio City. "You didn't forget the tickets, did you?"

I pull them out of my pocket and wave them in front of his face. "Not this time, Suedehead."

You can see the neon name of Radio City from blocks away, and it's something of a comfort, its simple existence. Last week my parents and I went through our photo albums, looking for pictures of the Twin Towers. We only found one, a blurry shot taken on the Staten Island Ferry, with me and my cousins in the foreground, horsing around. My aunt and uncle—in town from Florida—probably took many more shots of the skyline. It's an irony we're only now realizing—that out-of-towners probably have more photographs of the big things than we do. My first impulse when I see the red Radio City lights is to take a picture of them. Just in case.

We wait on line for security—something we're no doubt going to have to get used to—and then push into the crowded lobby. If you listen only to the noise, not the conversations, it's like nothing's happened. But when you get close enough to see the faces and hear the words, you're back in the post-9/11 world. It's only been a few weeks, but we know we're in a post-9/11 world. This isn't one of those changes when you wake up and wonder when it happened. We all know where the line was drawn.

It isn't until we get to our seats in the balcony that it becomes apparent that this sold-out show is not going to be a full one—there are hundreds of empty seats scattered around. People who no doubt didn't want to come into Manhattan. Or people who are afraid to be at Radio City, however improbable the threat.

We're a nervous, somber crowd. Then the lights go down,

and our concert instinct kicks in. Because there's still the unde-niable thrill of the silence before the opening chords, anticipa-tion turning into intensity, awaiting release. I am feeling an energy I don't fully understand, something that's been missing these past days and weeks.

The band comes on and launches right into "Sing," and we all rise to our feet and start singing along. John looks at me, and I look at him, and even though we both have awful voices, we shout our parts. And then there's "Writing to Reach You," and Fran Healy is singing, "My inside is outside / My right side's on the left side," and it's my favorite song of theirs and there is something so pure about a favorite song, and while it's always been a song about loving someone and will later be a song about loving someone, right now it's a song about confusion, and I am relating, because yesterday I used the word "tomorrow" when I meant to say "yesterday," and it made sense that I could feel that turned around. The whole crowd is relating, and it only escalates when the song ends and Fran shouts out, "Hello, New York!"

Three simple words, and there are tears in my eyes. He asks for the houselights to be turned on so he can see our faces, and even though he's way too far away to see mine and I'm way too far away to see his, it's still like I'm included. He says the band had discussed canceling the show, because they weren't sure any-one would come out for it. But they didn't cancel it, and they're here, and we're here, and we're all cheering, and then he says the thing that does me in, which is that there are six thousand of us here tonight, and I look around the room from the balcony and see all of the people here, and that number is just too painful, because right now, that's the number of people they're saying died in the World Trade Center—six thousand—and it's like suddenly Radio City Music Hall has been turned into a way station for ghosts, because I'm imagining all the people who died sitting in our rows, from the front row of the orchestra to the last row of the third balcony, and because of the gold-plated walls and the glowing lights and the red velvet chairs, it's both indescribably depressing and inexplicably magisterial. So many people. And after that flash of the dead, suddenly the crowd is the crowd again, and it's not the six thousand people who died, but six thousand other people, randomly joined by an affinity for this Britpop band, and I understand the energy I felt before but didn't have a name for—it's the energy of *gathering*, and the reason it's so striking is that none of us have gathered like this since 9/11, none of us have been a part of a crowd, none of us have acted out in unison in this way. We six thousand are cheering together. Standing together. The next song starts, and we're singing together. We all understand that this is just music. We all understand that these songs were written Before—there is no way the band could have known how we would hear them After. But the songs ring true. When Fran gets to "Side," he talks about how the globe is a sphere and has no sides. Introducing it, he says, "We all wake up in the morning, we all take a shit. It's just a few dickheads who fuck things up for the rest of us." And we're all clapping and yelling because in all the coverage we've been watching, nobody has said it so simply, and then backed it up with a song. When they get to "Why Does It Always Rain on Me?" we're laughing, because the woe-is-me lyrics have always been undercut by the jauntiness of the tune, and now we're realizing that the lyrics themselves have become more innocent. We're not afraid of rain anymore.

In the best concerts, the band is as moved as the audience, and this is the case tonight. We all realize that this gathering is about much more than the music, and what we're getting from it is much more than sounds. "I want to live in a world where I belong," Fran Healy sings in "Turn." Then, later on, "I want to live in a world where I'll be strong." Before when I listened to this, I would think about being gay, or about needing to be there for my friends, or even about more general things like being the main character in my own life. But now I realize it's even more general than that—it's about life itself. Fran promises it won't be very long, and we sing with him. Because we want to believe it. We want to believe the world will turn. We want to believe we'll survive.

The band plays and plays. The guitarist wears a John Lennon New York City T-shirt and belts out Bowie's "All the Young Dudes." Then Fran announces that the band is giving all the proceeds from the night's concert to the firefighters' fund, and we all go crazy. John is actually standing on his chair, screaming his cheers. We're all one voice now, this living gathering of six thousand. We are cheering, and we are speechless. We are happy, and we are crying. We are vulnerable, and we are strong. The band launches into a cover of "Happy," singing "I'm so happy / 'Cause you're so happy." We are jumping and dancing and cheering so much we can't see the empty seats. We can't hear the silences. We've become a part of the music. Not only the music that's being played. But the music of living.

I need that.

GROUND ZERO
Jasper

When my parents finally made it home, twelve days after 9/11, my mother grabbed hold of me and wouldn't let go. After all the nights of thinking they were going to come through the door without warning, I ended up meeting them at the airport. I stood in the sea of sons and daughters, craned my neck over the fathers and mothers, witnessed the procession of jet-weary travelers wheeling their carts from baggage claim. For once, the car-service drivers with their wipe-off name cards were in the minority. Family was here to see family return.

I had forgotten how small my mother was. Somehow, over the phone lines, I started seeing her again like I had when I was a kid. Had you asked me if I could fit in her lap, I would have said yes, of course. But now her head fell under my chin as she hugged me and hugged me and hugged me. Then she let go, and my father offered his hand. There was something misty in his expression, and even if he couldn't bring himself to embrace me in public, I was sure that he was glad that my mother had.

I wanted to pause us there, that faint triangle of bodies at the foot of an escalator. Because I knew it was inevitable that once we left that spot, one of us would say something stupid, and we would be annoyed with each other all over again.

They'd flown into Newark, so we had a long cab ride ahead of us. My mother asked me how the city was doing, as if it were a dying relative, and I asked how my grandmother was doing, and found out she wasn't going to die quite as soon as we thought. There wasn't much for me to tell them that I hadn't said in my mother's daily phone calls—there weren't many lengths of the censored version left to explore. I didn't tell them how, knowing that they were coming home the next day, I'd gone with two school friends to Splash the previous night, which ended up being a bad, bad idea. Splash was a tacky tourist gay-gay go-go bar on the best of nights, but on this particular night it was particularly gruesome. Some guys were sputtering around in a somber daze, like they'd just found out that porn wasn't the cure for cancer. I wanted to slap them for bringing us all down. But then there were the other guys, the ones whose heads were full of helium, who were prancing and dancing and romancing like this was the Best Week Ever, and they were having the Best Time Ever, and I wanted to slap them even more, because it didn't seem to be human to be having such fun. One of the guys hit on me—swooped right in, high on the drug of his choice, and he was like, "Hey, what's your name?" When I wasn't forthcoming with that particular piece of information, he followed up with the immortal "I love Asian men." And I was all, "What the fuck is your problem?"

and he came back with, "Hey, man, I was just trying to have a good time." I hated him at that moment—deeply—and part of that hate was raw envy. I wanted to be that oblivious. And sure, I drank enough that you would've thought I'd have gotten there, but the thing was, I never really drank to make myself happy. I only drank to match my sadness.

None of this was a story I wanted to tell my parents. So I let them give me the update on all of my Korean relatives. The narrative only stopped when we rounded a curve on the Pulaski Skyway and the Manhattan skyline suddenly came into view. My father saw it first, and without a word, he started to cry. A few one-at-a-time tears down his cheeks, quickly blotted away. My mother gasped, held her hand over her mouth. The smoke was gone. The fires were out. So what they were reacting to was the absence, the space. Because no matter how many times you saw it on TV, it was much more real when you looked out the window and saw it, just like you'd looked out the window so many times before and saw them there.

"Oh," my mother said. "Oh."

She held my father's hand, squeezed it, and he squeezed back.

I wanted to ask the cabdriver if this happened every time he hit this spot. If he was used to it now. If you ever got used to it.

It wasn't until my mother had let go of my father's hand that she reached for mine. As if she knew the three of us holding hands would be too much. As if we'd never be able to look each other in the eye after that.

I had seen the Twin Towers my whole life. But my parents had come here just before they were built. They had seen them rise. I wondered if that made a difference.

We went through the Holland Tunnel, then cut across on Canal Street to get to the Manhattan Bridge. Canal Street seemed to have returned to normal, with all the bargain stores selling knockoff purses and one-dollar batteries. I think this was the second shock to my parents—that things could have already resumed. They expected everything to have been altered. I didn't know how to explain to them that even if the stores were open and people were back on the street, something had shifted. We saw each other differently. I looked out of the cab window now at these strangers in a different way than I had looked out of the cab window at strangers before. I saw the gay boys at Splash a little differently. I saw the people on the subway ride home differently. Maybe it was just me who had changed, but I didn't think it was that. I thought it was everyone.

"I wish we had been here," my mother said, her voice reduced to a whisper.

I looked to my father, to see if he would nod, if he would agree. But he just stared out the window as we crossed the bridge, silently looking downtown, the latest in a long line of mourners.

The house was spotless. Like a Martha Stewart–sponsored archaeologist, I had managed to excavate the rooms, restoring them to what they once had been, before I'd laid my layers of in-somniac sediment on top of them. Even my own room was clean, the bed made, the papers I had gathered on 9/11 safely collected under a paperweight on my desk. It had to look like their home when they came back, not my home.

I only had two more days before I would be going back to school. The next morning, my father left for work before I got up. Because of everything that had happened, I strangely imag-ined him putting off the office for my last day home, even though I had no idea what we would have actually done with that time. Would he have gone school shopping with me and my mother? Would he have taken us out to lunch? Asked us if we wanted to see a movie? It was hard to picture, and even harder to picture wanting, but I still resented his cereal bowl, waiting in the sink for my mother to clean it. I resented that it probably hadn't occurred to him to stay.

My mother and I retraced last year's pre-college shopping, even though I already had most of what I needed. Shopping had always been something we could do together, much easier than sitting across a table and talking. Every aisle we walked down, there seemed to be at least three different things she said she could buy me. I wanted to tell her that there was no need to pay me off for leaving me alone on 9/11, no need to buy me things so I'd remember her when I was away. *I love you more than that,* I wanted to say, but there was no way to say it, because that wasn't the kind of thing my family said. It was all understood—or maybe it wasn't understood at all. There was no way to know.

All it took was three hours of shopping—of her insisting I get new sheets, of her asking if I wanted to get a haircut, of her telling me I needed to get "some good shirts" (the implication being that I had plenty of "bad shirts")—for me to be thoroughly exasperated. But the perverse thing was: I loved it. Because I realized that this had been one of the things I'd missed—this everyday feeling of having a family.

At lunch, my mother caught me looking at her.

"What?" she asked, touching her hair as if I was about to tell her it was out of place.

"I'm just glad you're back," I said.

She started to tear up.

"Aw, Mom," I said.

She wiped her eyes with a tissue.

"I'm glad I'm back, too," she said. "I just wish you were here longer."

I honestly couldn't imagine being around much longer. My college was notoriously one of the last to go back, so most of the people I knew had already gone back, once the roads and flyways were deemed safe again. Even the stores were acting like I was running late, displacing the back-to-school items for Halloween displays. (My mother had, in fact, asked if I wanted to get my costume now.)

I don't think it hit me until later that afternoon. My mother was napping off the time-zone shift and I was starting to pack up my bad shirts. I thought about turning on the news, and suddenly I wasn't thinking about it in terms of leaving for school—I was thinking of it in terms of leaving the city. And that felt wrong.

It nagged at me through dinner. My father, who had not napped and had found the usual incompetence at the office when he returned, was in a grumpy mood. My mother was trying to compensate for it. And I was paralyzed because all I wanted to talk about was what had happened in the days since 9/11, but I couldn't really talk about it with them, because they hadn't been here. And I realized that it would only be worse back at school, where I'd be surrounded by people who hadn't been here, who wouldn't understand. Or even if they had been here, like Amanda, they wouldn't understand what I'd felt, what I'd been through. The emptiness was returning, and nobody around me had the words to fill it.

I made it through dinner, but barely. I made excuses about having to pack, and I was released to my room.

Packing didn't really take long, since I'd left a lot of things in storage up at school. I wanted to go out, but not in a Splash sense. I felt the urge to wander, to walk the streets all night, to show up back on my doorstep an hour before my train was going to leave. I was caught in a fit of restlessness, but unlike most fits of restlessness, this one had a direction. I was denying it, but there was definitely a direction. I just didn't know if I had the courage to follow the arrows.

I waited until my parents had said good night—my father with a nod, my mother with a kiss. I waited until their light was out and the house was quiet. Then I grabbed my keys, left a note, and took the subway into Manhattan, getting off at City Hall and walking west. The streets were fairly empty; Wall Street was closed for the night. But as I got closer, there were more people.

Ground Zero was lit like a movie set. These gigantic spotlights were covering it all as people worked around the clock to sift through the debris. They were no longer looking for survivors. Now they were looking for clues—clues to what happened, clues to who was in there. DNA from the dust. Confirmation of what we already knew.

There was a fence up, and NYPD officers everywhere. There were tourists, ·people with cameras, snapping away. I wanted to tell them to stop. I wanted to tell them this wasn't an attraction. They were like spectators at an execution. I didn't care how far they'd come. There was no way a New Yorker would take pictures of this.

The New Yorkers were quiet. Some in clusters, some alone. We hung around the parameters, helpless. We knew we wouldn't find what we were missing here. We would only find something that was missing more.

There were still shards of the towers' exterior jagging from the ground, broken shell pieces, walls for nothing. I stared at the biggest piece and tried to picture the towers, tried to see how far back I could remember them. And it was like in order to do that, I had to become a kid again, because that's the World Trade Center I saw, the one that a seven-year-old would see when he stood at the base and looked up, those endless metal-stripe walls reaching for the sky, the top of the building impossible to see. I remembered waiting on line in the lobby. I remembered the elevator ride making my ears pop. I remembered a family birthday we had at Windows on the World, and how the windows were so narrow. I remembered searching for my house from the Observation Deck.

But that was all I could remember. It was pointless to try to remember more. I remembered looking at the skyline and seeing them there. So tall, and yet still reflecting the given light of day.

I wanted answers. Not to questions like *How could this happen?* or *What could've been done to stop it?* No, more like *What am I supposed to do now?*

I knew I had to get back, but I couldn't move.

"Hey," a girl's voice said to me.

I turned and saw this short-haired blonde in a white T-shirt and jeans. She looked vaguely familiar—but most city girls do.

"This is random," she went on, "but you were at Mitchell's party, weren't you? Right before?"

"Yeah," I said. "Hey." I still had no idea who she was.

"I knew you looked familiar. I'm Claire. We didn't actually talk much at Mitchell's—I just remember people from parties. It's one of my hidden talents."

"I'm Jasper," I said, afraid I'd told her this at Mitchell's party a million times and was now making a fool of myself for repeating it again. I could remember Peter pretty clearly, but this girl . . . not even the glimpse of a memory.

"Hi, Jasper." Her voice completely friendly.

"Hi, Claire." I tried to sound friendly back.

She looked like she was having the same kind of night I was having, following the same arrows. She looked like she hadn't slept well in weeks. It didn't make her less attractive, but made it a more detailed attractiveness, like an older woman's.

"So, you live around here?" she asked.

I shook my head. "Brooklyn. Park Slope. I'm leaving for school tomorrow, so I decided to . . . you know . . ."

"Check it out before you left? Makes sense."

At this point we were both looking Zero-ward, not at each other. Seeing the workers yell to each other. Seeing them drink from thermoses, wearing jackets too heavy for the temperature.

"Do you live around here?" I asked.

"Yeah. About ten blocks away. We weren't allowed to come back for a week. It was pretty bad. But not, you know, the worst."

"Do you come here often?"

She actually laughed. "I bet you say that to all the ladies."

"I didn't mean—"

"I know. Plus, I know you're not into the ladies. You were all over Peter at the party, if I remember correctly."

Oh, man. Here it was—the reckoning.

"You know Peter?" I asked.

"Yeah—he and I were on the paper with Mitchell before he graduated. That's why we were at his party."

I was guessing that she wasn't that close to Peter, or she would've known to stay far away from me.

"Look," Claire said. "I know it's almost midnight, and you probably have to get back to Brooklyn, but do you want to walk for a little? I should be home, too, but if I go home now, I'm going to be up half the night. If we talk, I'll probably be able to clear my head enough to go to bed."

I found myself saying, "Sure," not really knowing why.

As we headed off, a tourist asked Claire if she'd take a picture of him and his wife in front of the wreckage.

"Sorry, no," she said, and moved on.

We were silent for a couple of minutes, and I wondered what the point was, if we were going to be silent. Yes, it felt different than wandering alone. But it only added awkwardness. It was like I'd agreed to go on a blind date and found out that we were going to only interact using cue cards.

"Where are you taking me?" I asked.

"Battery Park?"

"Sounds good."

"Isn't it amazing how Century 21 is still here?" she said as we passed by the department store. "I mean, it was right across from the towers—isn't it incredible how the building could collapse without hitting the building right across the street? Of course, if it had been damaged, maybe they would have rebuilt it with dressing rooms. A store like that should have dressing rooms. Anyway—sorry—that was totally uncalled for. What's your story? I mean, where were you that day?"

So we shared our stories—me at home, her at school, looking for her mother. By the time we were done, we were at the water, on the edge of Battery Park. The Statue of Liberty gleamed at us, putting her green-metal stamp on the lights and darkness. I tried again to remember Claire from Mitchell's party, but couldn't. This was probably because I definitely look at boys more than girls. But it wasn't just that. I imagined that while I was busy flitting around, she had stayed solidly in one place. I would never remember someone like that.

But here we were, and as she talked, I found myself liking her. She reminded me of people I liked—friends at school who were unafraid to meander, who never did the mean things I expected from other people. In New York City, where openness can be offered so pretentiously, so deliberately, there was something unplanned about Claire's voluntary kindness, her need to walk and talk. I usually avoided people like this, because I didn't feel I could give them what they needed. But something about this night, this time, made me want to stay. It made me want to play my part, and not have it be playing a part at all.

"What happened when you got back to your apartment?" I asked. "I mean, was it okay?"

Claire nodded. "The only thing wrong, really, was the air. On the first day, we lasted an hour, and then my mom said we had to go back uptown for the night, that we couldn't be breathing it in. I couldn't believe her—but then I thought about my little brother, and him breathing in whatever was in the air, and I had to give in. They said it wasn't poisonous, but it smelled poisonous. So we waited a few more days, and when we moved back in, Mom put in all these air purifiers."

"God, I can't imagine. It was bad enough in Brooklyn."

"And what did you do during the day?"

"I did nothing. Absolutely nothing."

"I can't imagine that," Claire said. And it wasn't like she was disputing the fact that I had done nothing. It was just that it was the opposite of what she'd been doing and feeling.

She went on. "There's the drown of things and the swim of things, I guess. I've been going back and forth, back and forth. I feel the weight of it. And this bewilderment—how can something that doesn't have a form, doesn't have a definition, doesn't have words—how can it have such weight? And yet, there's the need to swim."

"Life goes on," I offered.

"Yeah, but you see, *Life goes on* is a redundancy. Life is *defined* by its going on."

She walked over to a bench, and I sat down next to her. The tourists weren't going down here so much, so it was almost like we had the whole area to ourselves. The Staten Island Ferry shuttled back and forth as we watched, so empty that it was almost like it was traveling just so we could see it and mark the time by its passage.

"Have you talked to people about this?" Claire asked me. "I mean, about what happened? I've tried, but it never works. I don't know what I want from it, but I'm never satisfied. I can't talk to my mom about it. And even my friends are strange to talk to, because they're all caught up in their own versions, and every time I bring it up, they make it about them. I even tried talking to this girl in my class, Marisol, who was with me that day, but it was like that was all we had in common, and she didn't really want to talk about it."

I almost forgot she'd asked me a question. Then she paused, and I said, "Oh. Me? I haven't really talked to anyone. I mean, most of my friends were already back at school. And even the ones who were here—I just wasn't in the mood. I mean, what's the point?"

This wasn't really a question meant to be answered, but Claire looked out to the water and gave it a shot.

"I think the point is to realize you're not alone."

If you were quiet, you could hear the waves. In Manhattan, you forget you're surrounded by water, because you so rarely see it or hear it or feel its pull. But right at the edge, the air gains the current and the undertow. The water is black, but it carries any light that crosses it.

I don't know if it was because I was leaving the next day. I don't know if it was because I knew her without really knowing her. But for whatever reason, I followed her then. If you'd asked me if I wanted to talk, I would have said no, I didn't want to talk. But she didn't ask. And suddenly I was talking.

"It doesn't feel like 'alone,' though," I said. Not looking at her, looking at the ferry as it receded from Manhattan. "Solitary, maybe. I don't know. I just didn't want to deal with people.

Even when I was around people, I didn't want to deal with them."

"And when did it stop?" Claire asked.

I looked at her. "What do you mean?"

"I mean, when did you start dealing again?"

"Right now? This minute? I don't know."

It almost sounded like a line, as bad as *Do you come here often?* But Claire didn't seem cynical about it, or even find it strange. She just kept talking.

"Do you know what I want to know?" she said. "I want to know why this is such a part of me. I want to know why this thing that happened to other people has happened so much to me. I keep looking for the lesson."

"The lesson?" I asked.

"I don't mean that God made this happen to teach us something. Or to teach *me* something. How monstrously selfish would that be? I just mean that if we go through this thing and it changes us so much, you have to hope that it changes us for the better, right? If goodness can't come from bad things, it makes bad things unbearable."

I didn't know what to tell her. I didn't believe in good coming from bad. If it happened, that was great. But I couldn't believe in it.

"And the worst thing," she continued, "is that there are moments when I look around at everybody, at the way we've been acting since that day, and I wonder if maybe we needed to be hurt. I don't mean that I wanted it to happen, or that it should have happened. But I think we were walking around like we were invincible. And maybe that's a bad way to live your life. Because you're not invincible. Nobody is. And maybe now that we've learned that, we'll be better."

"Or we'll bomb the shit out of Afghanistan," I couldn't help but say.

Claire nodded sadly. Then she turned to me and put her hand lightly on my leg. "I know," she said. "But maybe we won't. Maybe there's a way to keep us in this moment. Not the sad part. But the coming together part."

I had to tell her, "It's not going to last."

"No," she said, taking my hand now. "But what if it did? Because if you step back from it—think about it—the past couple of weeks have been remarkable. I mean, what if September 11th, 2001, ends up being one of the most inspiring days in human history?"

"You're insane," I said.

"No—let me finish. I'm not saying it wasn't unfathomably tragic. It's awful. Completely horrific. It keeps me up and leaves me feeling totally inadequate to face it. But if you think about how everyone reacted—if you read the paper about everything that happened in reaction to the tragedy—you can almost find the beauty of it. The terrorists—those nineteen people, with hundreds or maybe thousands behind them—did the worst thing that you can possibly imagine. But tens of millions of people did the right thing. Not just the people who helped at Ground Zero and all the firefighters and police officers and first-aid workers. Not even the people in the city who took people in or helped them out or prayed. Or the people around the world who took in stranded travelers and also prayed and acted nicer to the people around them because everyone in that moment felt so vulnerable. Even more than that. I think that if you were somehow able to measure the weight of human kindness, it would have weighed more on 9/11 than it ever had. On 9/11, all the hatred and murder could not compare with the weight of love, of bravery, of caring. I have to believe that. I honestly believe that. I think we saw the way humanity works on that day, and while some of it was horrifying, so much of it was good."

"That's totally fucked up," I said.

Claire squeezed my hand. "Maybe it is," she said. "But maybe it isn't. Didn't you feel it on that day? It was like everyone suddenly knew what mattered. Money didn't matter. Politics didn't matter. Tabloid news didn't matter. No—compassion mattered. Calm mattered. Respect mattered. Did it really take something of this magnitude to make us realize this? Yeah, I guess so."

I wanted to believe her. But I wasn't sure I could. Because, ultimately, isn't your belief in human nature a perfect reflection of your own nature? If I expected the best from people, wouldn't I have to expect the best from myself?

"Usually I'm the fucked-up one," I said.

"There's more than enough of it to go around," Claire assured me.

A family of six passed by, looking like they had gotten up seven hours early for the first Circle Line tour. The youngest boy—he couldn't have been more than six—had Mickey Mouse ears on.

"You should talk to your friend Peter," I said. "I'm sure he can tell you stories about me."

"Why?" It was clear from her face that she had no idea.

"We were supposed to go out on 9/11," I explained. "But we rescheduled for later in the week. It didn't go well. I was a mess."

"I'm sure it wasn't that bad."

"It was. That bad."

Usually I could compartmentalize a bad date into a two-minute anecdote and eventually forget it had ever happened. But this one was haunting me more. Not because I felt Peter and I should've hit it off—even under regular circumstances, I don't think it would have gotten that far. But I guess I regretted it had been such a clusterfuck.

"Have you talked to him since?" she asked.

"We've emailed a couple of times. None of his emails have started with 'Dear Antichrist,' so I guess that's a good sign."

"I haven't noticed your name carved in his arm, either."

"Another good sign."

I was about to ask her if she was seeing someone when there was a noise from behind us. Nothing too dramatic—probably just some machinery being moved. But we were both startled for a second, then felt silly for it the moment after.

107

Or at least I felt silly. Claire just looked wistful, facing the lights at Ground Zero.

"I guess it's a choice we make," she said.

"What's a choice?" I asked.

And she said, "How much of the world we let in."

CATCHING BREATH
Claire

"What do you mean?" Jasper asks.

I don't know what I mean. I'm just talking. Words to find words. Words searching for words.

"I think it's something we all do," I say. "Not consciously, all the time. But we choose how much of the world we want to let into our lives. Both the beauty of it and the horror of it. There has to be a point of insulation—but some of us insulate real close, right down to our very selves, and others insulate wider, let more of the world in."

"And now?"

"Well, now the world has forced its way in. And once it retreats, we have to decide whether we put the insulation line in the same place or whether we move it out or in. I think I want to move it out. I want to include more of the world, even though I'm scared to."

I expect him to dodge what I'm saying—I sense he's an expert dodger—but instead he says, "I think I've been trying to draw it tighter. Not the world—the insulation."

"That's a natural enough thing to do," I tell him.

"I guess. If you want to be an asshole."

It is so strange to be here, to finally be saying all these things out loud. Some of them are things I didn't even know that I knew. And others are things I've wanted to pull people aside and say, but it was never the right time. My mother is on edge enough, trying to figure out our apartment and her job and whether living downtown is going to kill us. And maybe one of my friends at school would get it, but I haven't found which one yet. So here I am, with a near stranger, who John told me had hurt Peter's feelings, but not too bad.

"I want to tell you something," I say. And I'm not even sure what I'm going to tell him. I want to find the thing I most don't want to say, the thing I am the most unsure of, because I don't know if I'm going to have this chance again.

He opens the door. "What?"

And I'm telling him.

What?

I'm saying

"I liked breathing it in."

And he doesn't get it. So I say

"That air. The air afterwards. I wanted to breathe it in. It felt right to breathe it in. Because we were breathing them in, weren't we? And the buildings. We were breathing it all in. And I thought, there's a part of this that's actually a part of me now. I now have that responsibility. I am alive, and I am breathing, and I can do the things this dust can't do."

I think for the twelfth time tonight he's going to tell me I'm insane. But instead he says, "I collected their papers. The ones that blew into Brooklyn. They were just there at first. I didn't even know what they were. But once I did, I went all over the place, picking them up. I don't know what to do with them. I mean, they're meaningless now, but they still exist. You can't throw out something like that. You can't make them gone like that."

"You did the right thing," I say.

"For the first time in my life," he jokes.

"Not really," I tell him. "Not at all, I'm sure."

I'm not just saying it. I know it's true.

"Do you always have such faith in strangers?" he says.

"Only the ones who go out on really bad dates with my friends."

Wouldn't it be funny, though, if the answer was yes?

I want to have faith in strangers. I want to have faith in what we're all going to do next. But I'm worried. I see things shifting from United We Stand to God Bless America. I don't believe in God Bless America. I don't believe a higher power is standing beside us and guiding us. I don't believe we're being singled out. I believe much more in United We Stand. I have my doubts, but I want it to be true. Wouldn't it be wonderful if we really came together, if we really found a common humanity? The hitch is that you can't find a common humanity just because you have a common enemy. You have to find a common humanity because you believe that it's true.

It's getting cold out, and I don't have a jacket. I was only going to walk around for a few minutes. I just needed to say good night to the streets before going back to my room. I know I won't be able to keep doing this. I know the streets don't care. But I need to do it.

I shiver, and Jasper puts his arm around me. Not like a boy who's after a grope, or even a consoling parent. He just draws me a little into his body, making us a shelter for a time.

"I don't want to go," he says. "I mean, I can't stay in my house, and I'm sure school will be great, but at the same time, I don't want to go."

"The city will still be here, I promise," I say.

"But will it be the same city?"

I shake my head. "It's never the same city. Your city isn't even the same as my city, I bet."

"I guess."

"And that's not really the problem," I say.

"Then what is?"

"You don't want to deal. With life. With other people."

"You should've warned me you had a photographic memory."

"Can you have a photographic memory for things that are said? Wouldn't that be something else? And it was only a few minutes ago. Don't give me too much credit."

The funny thing is, I want to talk to him as much as he wants to talk to me. And I *have* been dealing. I've been going to school, doing my work, volunteering as much as I can, trying to get other people to volunteer, too. But I guess it's just as easy to get lost in the dealing as it is to get lost in the avoidance.

"Do you remember Mitchell's party?" Jasper asks.

"It seems like ages ago," I tell him. "But yes, I do."

"Tell me what you remember."

It's easy to know where to begin. "You were the life of the party," I say. "I mean, there wasn't a song you wouldn't dance to. Even the sappy ballads, you were swaying. I think you were wearing a blue shirt. I remember at one point you sat on Peter's lap. You were such a flirt. And he had such an instant crush on you."

"What else?" His eyes are closed, like he's a kid and I'm telling him a fairy tale.

"God, I don't know. I wasn't even going to go, but my friend Casey really wanted to go because she thinks Mitchell's brother, Bill, is really hot. So we got there, and it ended up that Bill was away wherever Mitchell's parents were. So Casey wanted to leave immediately, but I figured that since we were there, we should stay. Mitchell was always one of my favorite people in school. And, let's see, that night he was wearing a Nelly Furtado T-shirt, but he'd crossed out the Furtado part, so it just said Nelly. There might have even been some sequins involved. Am I right?"

Jasper nods, eyes still closed.

"And—I don't know—we were all really happy, weren't we? I mean, school had started, but the real part hadn't started yet. This was like the one weekend when we didn't have to worry about homework or colleges or SATs or anything. It was just a big welcome back. And Laine Taylor had cut all her hair off, and

Greg Watson had grown his long, and Aiden Smith couldn't stop talking about this guy who was a counselor with him who he'd fallen head over heels in love with. And Jill Breslin—God, poor Jill Breslin—she was drunk off her ass. On Bud Light! She was still really tan from the summer. She had on a necklace I really liked, although now I couldn't tell you what it was. Only that I liked it."

I want Jasper to chime in, but he just says, "What else?"

"What else?" I think about it. "I tried putting on some Tori Amos, but Mitchell said it wasn't party music and switched it back to Christina Aguilera. I asked him if he had any Ricky Martin. I was joking, and he said, 'Yeah, I have some Ricky Martin . . . in my bedroom.' Oh God—and then there was the fight that Greg and Lauren got into, about what time she had to be home. And he was saying they were seniors now, so her parents needed to let her stay out later than eleven on a Saturday, and somehow it became about how he doesn't understand her at all, and she was crying, and he was asking her what he did wrong, why she was acting like this, and the rest of us were like, 'There's no way I'm going anywhere near that.'"

"Good policy."

"I know!"

"What were you wearing?"

"I don't remember." I say that, and then I do remember. Not because I can picture myself wearing it, but because it was waiting for me in the hamper when we finally got back to the apartment. "Wait—it was a Sleater-Kinney T-shirt. And jeans."

114

I want Jasper to say he remembers me, he remembers the shirt. But it's clear he doesn't.

He opens his eyes. "I want to remember it more," he says. "The party. Because, you know, that was the last time."

"The last party of Before."

"Exactly."

I tell him I want to know if that girl—the one who was wearing the Sleater-Kinney T-shirt and (I remember now) flirting with Eric McCutcheon—is really all that different from who I am now.

"I have no idea," Jasper says.

"Well, neither do I. Obviously."

I realize something then: It's been at least a few minutes since I've noticed where I am. Which sounds like such a small thing, but lately it's been impossible. New York City disappeared, and I was inside the conversation.

"Remind me again," I say, "how the two of us ended up on this bench?"

I want to stay up all night talking. I want to start at Battery Park and walk a ring around Manhattan. But I know he has to go. I don't want to ask him to stay, because I don't want him to feel bad for having to leave.

So I'm the one who says it. I'm the one who says it's time to go. I'm the one who gets us up from the bench, who unwinds our words back to the subway, who pauses there for the moment of parting.

"This has been—" he says. Then stops.

We hug goodbye. I watch him go. And after he does, there's that brutal loneliness, that final period at the end of all the sentences. Then I step into the street, and another sentence. The loneliness lifts a little. If we'd talked at Mitchell's party, it would have never happened like this. Something opened us. And we needed to find each other open.

I unlock my front door. I walk up the stairs. I open our apartment door and tread lightly on the floorboards. I am home. I peek into my brother's room to see him sleeping. I listen to hear if my mother is awake, and silently say good night when I don't hear anything.

I go into my room. I imagine Jasper heading back on the subway. I change into my pajamas and turn off the light. I look at the window, the clock, the pillow.

I breathe it all in.

HOLD DEAR

(Part Four)

LOVE IS THE HIGHER LAW
Peter

The best concert of my life so far?

U2. Madison Square Garden. October 27, 2001.

And it's not like U2 was my favorite band or anything. I thought "With or Without You" and "I Still Haven't Found What I'm Looking For" were incredible, mind-twisting, truth-laid-bare songs. But other than that, Bono had never really reached me. When *All That You Can't Leave Behind* came out in November 2000, I loved "Beautiful Day" and liked the rest of the album. But it was just an album. I appreciated it, but didn't need it.

September changed that.

The song I latched onto most, the song that I would play ten times in a row because I needed to hear it all ten times, was "Walk On." It was that unexpected, almost religious thing: the right song at the right time.

And it wasn't because they were big rock stars. Instead it was the opposite of that. I think one of the reasons they've spoken to so many Americans right after 9/11 is because they know what we're going through. They lived through Ireland in the '70s and the '80s. They know what it's like to be bombed and threatened and afraid. They know what it's like to walk on. They're not just singing it.

Plus, it's somehow more touching to have a band that isn't American caring so much about us. We see Bono on the Tribute to Heroes concert, or touring around, and we know that people outside in the world care about us.

While I love "Walk On," my friend Claire holds close to "Stuck in a Moment You Can't Get Out Of" —

> *You've got to get yourself together*
> *You've got stuck in a moment and you can't*
> *   get out of it*

"That's it, isn't it?" Claire says as we head into the Garden. "That's what it's been like."

"Walk On" and "Stuck in a Moment You Can't Get Out Of." One song for moving, one song for stasis. Both songs fitting the times.

I asked Claire to come to the concert with me because we've become much closer over the past month. Strangely, it was Jasper717 who pointed her in my direction. I mean, Claire and I were already friends. But one day, out of the blue, she came right up to me at my locker and said, "Let's talk about what's going on." And at first I didn't understand what she meant, but then she was telling me how she was having trouble sleeping, and she asked me where I'd been on the morning of 9/11, because she remembered I wasn't there. Suddenly we went from being casual friends to being part of each other's lives—I don't know how else to explain it. Within a week, we'd made each other NYC Survival mixes—mine with "Walk On" and "Life Is Beautiful" and the Magnetic Fields' "The Book of Love," which isn't about survival at all, but is about why we would want to survive. And she had "Stuck in a Moment You Can't Get Out Of" and Dave Matthews performing "Everyday" acoustically and this song by a singer-songwriter named Cindy Bullens. I'd never heard it before, and I assumed it had been written about 9/11. But later Claire told me, no, it was actually from an album she wrote after her daughter died, and while it's one of the most startling, grieving albums I've ever heard, it also gives a kind of road map for survival. The song—"Better Than I've Ever Been"—begins:

> There's been a lot of things said about me
> Since that awful day
> I'm not the person that I used to be
> And that I'll never be the same
> That's true—no doubt
> But I know more now what life is about
>
> I laugh louder
> Cry harder
> Take less time to make up my mind
> and I

Think smarter
Go slower
I know what I want
And what I don't
I'll be better than I've ever been

It's become a kind of shorthand for me and Claire. "Laugh louder," I'll tell her. "Think smarter," she'll tell me. And "love deeper"—a lyric from later in the song.

I know U2 decided to call their tour the Elevation Tour long before current events became current, but it's still amazing how well it articulates what we're hoping for as the lights go down and Bono takes the stage. From the very first song, we feel it—all twenty thousand of us feel it. As U2 tears through the anthems—there's something in that word, *anthem*—we rise up to meet the music. We're not just a crowd. We're not just a gathering. We're a congregation.

Then the band gets to "One." As Bono sings, the names of all of the 9/11 victims are projected onto the backdrop of the stage. All of those names. And the song transforms into something much bigger than it is. And we transform into something much bigger than we are. We are crying and holding on to each other and singing along and reading, reading, reading.

All of the names, as we're told love is the temple, love is the higher law. Who can look at this list of names and not imagine himself or herself on it? Who can't try to picture what that must be like for friends or family? Some of the names are familiar—

not because I know the person, but because I know someone else with that name. And some of the names are familiar because every day I read the page in the *New York Times* that they devote to telling a brief life story of every single person who died in the attacks. A life is in the details, not the statistics, and every day I learn how one person who died met his wife, or how another who died chose the name for her son. It's more than a list, because the details add the music. And now I feel I am actually remembering instead of simply memorializing. As accurate or inaccurate as that might be.

If you start the day reading the obituaries, you live your day a little differently. I have been thinking about the people in my life, and how much more I want them to be in my life. Like Aiden, my first boyfriend. I find myself struck with such fondness for our first fumblings, for the sureness that sometimes spills over into arrogance. I've talked with him more in the past few weeks than I had in months. Because he's a part of my history, and part of my present.

And then there's Claire, standing beside me. As "One" crescendos and we all leave our feelings bare, she and I are both crying. And while usually I'm embarrassed to cry in public, there's no room for embarrassment here. I look at Claire and think, *I want to know you for a long, long time.* I want us to be able to share the details we find in obituaries, and the songs that cover the wide terrain of our moods, and the words that come easily, and the words that don't. Because that's what friendship is to me right now. What I share with this arena of strangers is one thing, and what I share with Claire is another. Both are essential. Both are part of that higher law.

We are face to face with enormity again, but this time we are going to make it through. It is a moment we can get out of. Together.

DECEMBER 4, 2001
Jasper

I went the whole day without thinking about it. Exams. Exes.
Roommate issues—that's what filled my day. I didn't let the
world in at all. Or that day.

Until, of course, the end of the day, when I realized I had
gone the whole day without thinking about it, and wondered
what that meant.

THE LIGHTS
Claire

The swim of things. Leaves falling on sidewalks like autumn garlands. Candy corns and the way the light turns crisp as winter approaches. Playground voices. Conversations about favorite movies, favorite books. Friends. New Year's. A snowman on the sidewalk. Reading a story to your little brother before he goes to sleep.

Holding dear. Realizing the difference between *things* and *possessions* is that possessions are the things that are dear to you. Realizing, with this word *dear*, that things are dear to me. Discovering how dear life is. Same word—slightly different meaning. That twist of fragility.

The weight does not lift itself, although over time it lightens. Sometimes we need to push. And sometimes that is very hard.

It is still strange to see the skyline. I have never seen an absence that's so physical. It's possible I will see the absence for the rest of my life, even when there is something else there. Which is okay. The thing to remember when looking at an absence is that you are standing outside of it.

We still feel some things in common. And we still feel some

things that are entirely our own. I can only say what I'm feeling, and even that is only the fraction that I can articulate at any given moment. I still have those childish moments when I wish with all my heart that I could wake up and find it's all been a dream. I really have thought that. I have felt—stronger than grief, stronger than anger, stronger than despair—the profound desire to return to the netherworld of the safer past. There are still the flashes of unexpected sadness, the pauses that last longer than they used to. The desire for retribution, the fear of retribution. Like a death in the family, like a personal tragedy, an event like this lays bare the complexity of our worlds, internal and external.

But you can't live life in the shadow of all that. I think about the posters, how they went in a matter of days from posters of the missing to posters of the missed. Eventually they were taken down. Gone is not forgotten, but our lives cannot be a memorial. This city cannot be a memorial. This city has to be a city. Our lives have to be our lives.

The swim of things. I go on an airplane. I walk under the Empire State Building. I take the bus, and the subway, and am surrounded by strangers the whole time. I certainly have room in my life for caution, but I have no room in my life for paralyzing fear. There's always a risk. There always has been. But I'd rather live my life than die of negations.

There is not one moment when that feeling of inadequate sorrow goes away. It just lessens and lessens, until it is mostly a memory of itself.

127

We live in the same apartment. I go to the same school. I apply to college. I get into college.

Somehow, six months pass.

I'm not at home when they light the lights.

I'm at school, finishing up our environmental club newsletter. I'm the last one there besides the janitors, and it's dark out when I finally leave. It's March 11 and I have been aware of the anniversary all day, but I still gasp when I look downtown and see the beam of blue light coming from where the towers used to be. I feel such a silence pass through me. Ghosts.

I know what I have to do. And suddenly it's the opposite of that day. Because instead of walking away, I am walking toward. Instead of taking my brother's hand and heading north of Fourteenth Street, I am alone and heading home. The towers have been resurrected as spirits, and I am going to visit them. In the chilly night-darkness, they are their own beacon. All I have to do is go down the street and face the right way. There they are. Alighting over the tops of the SoHo buildings. Hiding behind streetlamp glare, arching over our heads. I keep walking. I keep following. Past Canal Street. Past Duane.

I still find it hard to see Ground Zero. I still find it hard to witness the nothingness. The lights are not a remedy for this. There will never be a remedy for this. But they are a strikingly apt presence. They are both something and nothing at once. They fill the space without claiming it as their own. They are translucent. They blur.

I walk down the nearly empty West Side Highway. I walk past Stuyvesant, toward the pedestrian bridge we all saw on TV that day. I think of turning back. I'm not sure I can do it. I have been so good about getting back to normal, about moving on, about forgetting enough so the pain doesn't keep me awake, but remembering enough so that I am a different, better person. The lights keep drawing me on. Because I know that in a short time they will be gone. And I know I have to experience them before they disappear.

I reach the base. It's not at Ground Zero—it's a few blocks over, surrounded by offices that were untouched that day. You can see the buildings right through the lights. Each beam is made of dozens of singular rays that seem, at the bottom, entirely like the latticework of the towers. There are not many people at the base—mostly families, the children running around as if they're at a playground, a light show. I don't mind their laughter or their chatter; it's a nice juxtaposition against the size of the moment, like having a baby make noise at a funeral. I face skyward, tracing the intersection of seeming parallels. Light like specters and souls and geometry. Towers of lights of towers.

I walk to the edge of the lights and see Ground Zero, see Century 21. I could just go home. I could call it a night.

But something about the lights has emboldened me. I head west. Frightened.

This is something I haven't told anyone. Not Peter. Not my mom. Not Jasper. Even though I pass by Ground Zero almost every day, I still have been too afraid to go to Rockefeller Park. It's a small stretch of park along the Hudson, and it's always been one of my favorite places in New York, one of those magical corners that you feel is your own even though you share it with thousands of people. I knew it wasn't part of Ground Zero—I knew it was probably okay—but still I hadn't tried to see it. I hadn't wanted to see it any different, was afraid I would find it cordoned off or shifted over to rubble. When buildings collapse, why respect a park?

But tonight it's time. I walk around Stuyvesant. I turn the corner. I hold my breath. I look. And it's still there. Every railing. Every step. Everything.

When I hit the water's edge, I turn south, toward the plaza. Because seeing the park...seeing the Jersey ferry dock...suddenly I know what I have to find. My favorite piece, the railing directly outside the World Financial Center, the one inscribed with a quote from Walt Whitman and a quote from Frank O'Hara—quotes I have not been able to remember. I've only been able to remember how much I loved them. I have always loved them, always made a point to walk by them, always assumed they'd always be there. And since 9/11, I'd assumed they'd been destroyed in everything that had happened.

As I turn to walk south, I am sure in my bones that the railings won't be there. As I walk closer, I think it might be possible that they've survived. As I turn and see the Financial Center's plaza, hurt but still standing, I think it's very possible, but still I can't believe it. Nearer and nearer. I see part of it is blocked off. Then I can see it. Right there. And I am so happy and so sad at the same time. I am exuberant and despondent and utterly, completely beside myself. There they are. And I know it's ridiculous—with so many dead, so much destroyed that I can feel so much joy over a series of metal letters affixed to a metal railing. Life ends, and life goes on. Words disappear, and words remain. I can stand along the water as an orchestra of wind envelops me. I can feel the same things I used to feel as this happened, and I can feel other things ghostlike beside them. I can look to the skyline, and where I once saw twin towers, I can now see twin lights. I cannot begin to understand how this works.

I write the railing quotes on the back of an envelope, so I will never lose them again.

CITY OF THE WORLD (FOR ALL RACES ARE HERE, ALL THE LANDS OF THE EARTH MAKE CONTRIBUTIONS HERE), CITY OF THE SEA! CITY OF WHARVES AND STORES—CITY OF TALL FACADES OF MARBLE AND IRON! PROUD AND PASSIONATE CITY—METTLE-SOME, MAD, EXTRAVAGANT CITY!
—WALT WHITMAN

ONE NEED NEVER LEAVE THE
CONFINES OF NEW YORK TO
GET ALL THE GREENERY ONE
WISHES—I CAN'T EVEN ENJOY
A BLADE OF GRASS UNLESS
I KNOW THERE'S A SUBWAY
HANDY OR A RECORD STORE OR
SOME OTHER SIGN THAT PEO-
PLE DO NOT TOTALLY REGRET
LIFE.

—FRANK O'HARA

AFTER

(Part Five)

A REUNION
Peter

Even though I know they've kept in touch, it doesn't occur to me that Jasper will be at Claire's birthday party. But here he is, looking both hot and sheepish when he sees me. Our email exchange trickled to nothing in the fall, and I honestly never thought I'd see him again. Or if I did, I didn't think it would be like this, with me all nervous and wondering what to do.

Claire must know this, because she comes over and says, "Here, I'll try to make it less awkward." And the sweet thing about Claire is that she's wrong about half the time when it comes to social interactions, but she's well intentioned and kindhearted enough that you don't really mind; if anything, you try to bend the situation to meet her intentions, so she won't be disappointed.

"I believe you two know each other," she says, dragging me over.

"Hey," he says.

"Hey," I say.

It's not like I think of him often. If anything, he's just this weird romantic-but-not-really footnote to a really big milestone.

He's just come in, and he hands Claire an elaborately wrapped present.

"You don't have to open it now," he says.

"I'm opening it now," she replies, not tearing into the paper as much as unfolding it. There are many layers—and I realize what he's done. Each layer is the front page of a Monday newspaper, so with each layer Claire peels back, she's going back a week. May. April. March.

There's an envelope at the center—a photo envelope from CVS.

"I didn't take them myself," he says. "But one of my friends was here for break, and he took them, and I thought you'd want to have them. To remember."

The photos are of the lights. Some shaky, some crystal clear. Some up close so you can see every beam, and some from far away—Brooklyn or Jersey—so you see the blue shoot up from the skyline.

"Oh, Jasper," Claire says, hugging him. And even I want to tell him that he's done a good job. I doubt she'll like my birthday present (another mix, *Eighteen Songs for Eighteen Years*) half as much.

More people come in, and Claire needs to be social. Her little brother is answering the door, dressed in a shirt and tie—a regular gentleman, unlike the rest of us.

Why is it so awkward? We shared one night—two, if you count Mitchell's party. It shouldn't matter to see him. It should be fine.

"So how've you been?" Jasper asks. His hair is a little longer in the front. There's no reason Claire would've told me that.

"I don't know," I say. "Good."

We fall into the usual conversational pattern—he asks me where I'm going in the fall, and I tell him which school, and he says it's only an hour from his school, and I don't know what to say to that, so he quickly says he has friends at my school and that they all love it there.

"What are you doing for the summer?" I ask him.

"I'm actually going to Korea for a couple of months," he tells me. "I'm trying to brush up on my international relations. Plus, my grandmother keeps almost-dying on us, so my mom and I are going to stay with her for a while. I used to dread the three weeks we went in the summer, and now I'm going for nine weeks. Go figure. And what about you? What are you doing this summer?"

I shrug. "Hanging around here mostly. Saying goodbye. Getting ready for school. Claire's dragging me down to Arkansas to build houses for a week. But other than that, I'm around."

There's really no reason for us to still be talking to each other. There are dozens of other people I know here. I could be talking to them. And yet we keep talking. Like there's a point we need to reach.

"So what else is new?" he asks.

I find myself saying, "I have a boyfriend now."

He smiles and says, "Of course you do." Then he adds, "I mean, you should. You're great boyfriend material."

"He's actually the first guy I ever kissed," I tell him. "Aiden."

"I bet he has more body hair now," Jasper says.

"Uh . . . I guess he does."

"I'm sorry. That was random. And I haven't even had a drink yet."

"No worries."

Jasper shakes his head. "You're too forgiving. I still owe you an in-person apology for that awful date."

"It's okay," I tell him. "It was a surreal time. Remember how we kept using that word? *Surreal?* Well, it was. Nobody is accountable for their actions then. And nothing really happened."

"I know. But still."

I put my hand on his arm.

"Really," I say. "It's okay."

He looks at me then, and it's weird, because even though I don't really know him, I know he's different now, too. Maybe it's just because of the things Claire's told me. Or maybe I can actually see it.

At this point I feel arms snaking around me from behind, then feel a kiss on the side of my neck.

"Hey, boyfriend," Aiden says.

"Hey, Aiden," I say.

I make introductions, but I know the introductions are only going to lead to outroductions. Jasper doesn't want to meet Aiden. Aiden doesn't want to meet Jasper. And I don't particularly want them to meet each other. As soon as the hellos are over, Jasper says he sees Mitchell in the corner, and that he should go say hi.

That's it. We're done. He leaves about an hour later. He goes out of his way to say goodbye to me, but it's just goodbye.

OF COURSE YOU HAVE A BOYFRIEND
Jasper

When I said "Of course you do," I meant this:

Of course you have a boyfriend, because right now my deepest wish is that you don't have a boyfriend. Because even though I haven't seen you in almost a year, and even though the last time we were in a room together was one of the most awkward mornings of my life, now that we're talking again, it feels like we should be talking, it feels like this should be part of something, and maybe it's because Claire is always telling me how wonderful you are, and maybe it's because that shirt does something to your eyes, and maybe it's because when you have a boyfriend, it releases these strange pheromones that unwittingly attract foolish boys like myself. I don't know. Maybe it's because even though our first date was one of the biggest messes I've been party to, it was also one of the most intense dates I've ever been on, and I used to think that it was entirely because of the events of the week, but now I'm wondering if maybe you and I didn't have something to do with it, too. And maybe it scared me that you were still in high school, but you're not in high school anymore, and will in fact be within an easy train or bus ride to my school. And maybe it's the fact that Claire loves us both, and that we both love Claire, and that even though neither of us will ever be with Claire in a boyfriend way, maybe the fact that we can both be on her wavelength so well means we could be on each other's wavelength, too. Or maybe I'm just desperate because everybody I meet is either too gloomy or too happy— never a good balance of the two. Maybe it's because I'm leaving for Korea in three days, and if I'm going to see you again, I know it has to be in the next three days. Or maybe the fact that you have a boyfriend has nothing to do with me. I mean, I know it has nothing to do with me. And I can't help but wish, in this very specific moment, that it did have something to do with me.

But none of this is what I said next. Instead I went with:

"I mean, you should. You're great boyfriend material."

In other words, I kept digging the hole.

GOOD NIGHT (YOUR MORNING)
Jasper

5/31/02

Greetings from JFK. Before I leave the country, I wanted to let you know that it was really
good to see you at Claire's party. Part of me
wishes that there would have been a way for
us to meet for the first time there. I think we
would have had more to talk about if we'd
been strangers with a kick-ass wonderful
mutual friend.

Plane's boarding soon. Gotta go.

Take care,
J.

6/29/02

I think my grandmother is addicted to uppers.
Or maybe she just spikes her tea with Red
Bull. I don't understand it. From everything
my parents told me, I was expecting this
frail, sickly woman. But my grandmother is

unstoppable. If it weren't for my internship, I swear she'd be taking me on the town every hour of every day, and most of every night, too. She doesn't speak more than ten words of English, so all the Korean I've been blocking out is coming back again. Every now and then she puts on what I like to call her "Truth Face"—when it appears, I know she's going to lean over and impart some wisdom to me, usually culled down to a single line. She repeats them a lot. Some have to do with hygiene, which I won't repeat here (except to say that soap is important, but water is *more* important). Her favorite, though, is this:

The secret to living long is to have something to live for.

She's eighty-seven, so I'm guessing this is something she's put some thought into. Or maybe it's just something she found on a greeting card and liked. Who knows? The best part is that a lot of the times when she says this, she follows up by telling me she's happy I'm around. I'm her only grandchild, you know. I feel such responsibility. But that's okay.

How's Life After High School?

Take care,
J.

7/25/02

I wish I was building houses right now with you and Claire. I can't stand the fact that the two of you don't have email for a week. I know I'm a gazillion miles away, but I miss you. I miss finding your words in my inbox. (No, that's not a euphemism.)

It's amazing to live in a divided country. I mean, I've heard about it all my life—my dad has relatives that ended up in North Korea while the rest of the family was in South Korea. But I don't think I really appreciated what it meant until now. I mean, it's like New York and Connecticut had this huge falling-out and suddenly nobody from Connecticut was allowed to go to New York, and vice versa. It's one thing to think of it in political terms, as part of the story of the Cold War. But when you start thinking of it in human terms, it blows your mind.

Please thank Claire for teaching me to think in human terms. Although I'm sure she'll give some of the credit to everyone else.

Yours from far, far away,
J.

I'm sorry to hear about you and Aiden. That's rough. Even if you wanted it to happen, there's always the actuality of it happening, which is never entirely what you imagine it will be.

I think my mom and I are both ready to come home. Not only because my grand-mother is completely running us ragged, but because it feels like we've been living a life separate from our real lives. We actually talked about it last night. She told me how much she missed my father. And it's strange, because that actually surprised me, since I don't miss him at all, or at least not that much. But I forget that she has made her life with him, while I've moved on to college. And that they probably have a whole separate life to themselves that I rarely see. It's weird to think about. I found myself telling her how much I missed you and Claire, and how we've been writing practically every day. She asked if you were friends from school, and I had to try to ex-plain to her that, no, you're just these two people I met and kept. I'm not sure she un-derstood, but she might have. Whatever the case, my mom now knows about you. Isn't it time you told your mother about me? (Just kidding.)

It does bum me out that you'll be gone by the time I get home. At the same time, we're not too bad at mastering the time-space continuum, are we? (Sorry if I geeked you out there.)

Good night (your morning),
J.

P.S.—I'm actually not sorry at all to hear about you and Aiden. I'm actually quite selfishly happy.

P.P.S.—I'm going to hit send before I delete that last P.S.

8/21/02

Absolutely. It's time.

Love,
J.

HERE TO YOUR THERE
Peter

6/4/02

it's great to hear from you, jasper. i hope korea is treating you well. i've never been there, but you probably would have guessed that. things here are good. school is winding up. aiden was really mad because i took claire to the prom. not because i didn't want people to know i was dating aiden—he's very public in his affection, so i think it's safe to say that everyone already knows. it's just that i promised claire i would take her, back in october. you might already know this, but on our way home from a concert, she asked me to the prom, made me promise we'd decorate each other's mortarboards for graduation, and signed me up for habitat for humanity this summer, all at once. she said she wanted to make sure this would be our year, and i wasn't about to argue with her. aiden doesn't get it. i bet you do.

anyway, we had a blast. i think graduation's going to be very emotional—even more emotional than usual. because it's been one hell of a year.

tell me more about korea,
peter

7/5/02

the 4th of july was a little bit of overkill this year, i have to say. i think i'm getting tired of flags. at first, i didn't mind how they sprang up everywhere, because it was a sign of unity. but now it's turned into this weird patriotism contest. and that's not the point, is it?

claire's worried about war. she says hi.

here to your there,
peter

8/5/02

we're back, and soon you'll be back (although i'll be off to orientation by then). building a house was an incredible experience—at the risk of sounding like claire, it's pretty incredible to do something so concrete for total strangers. at one point they had this t-shirt contest, where we were all supposed to come up with a phrase for our t-shirts, and

claire won it with this simple phrase—
"strangers are neighbors"—that completely
summed it up.

in other news, there was this boy there, clay-
ton, who was totally in love with claire. she
denies it completely, but she blushes every
time i bring it up. i hope they write.

in other, other news, of a less blushworthy
variety (unless it's a blush of embarrassment), aiden and i finally called it quits. i think
he was waiting until i got back from arkansas
because he didn't want me to be bummed
out while i was there, but the truth is that although that's a sweet thing to do, i don't actually know how bummed out i would've been.
college was going to break us up anyway, but
i'm glad it was clear that it wasn't just college.
i'm sad, but not too sad. i'm more sad that it
went on for so much longer than it should
have, you know?

claire and i are going to koreatown for dinner
tonight. because we know you spent the last
week going to arkansas restaurants, just to
be with us.

we'll raise a toast,
peter

8/20/02

okay, we've exchanged at least thirteen thousand emails without coming out and saying
it, and since i'm leaving tomorrow, i'm going
to come right out and say it.

it's about time for our second date, isn't it?

have a safe flight tomorrow,
peter

ANNIVERSARY
Claire

I think I'll retrace my steps—but there's too much that's happened in the year. There is no way to do it. I'm in college now, still in the city, but part of a lifetime away from Mrs. Otis's classroom. There's no way to be standing where I'd been standing, no way to go to Mrs. Lawson's classroom and stay with her and Sammy. We think that time is the only thing that passes, but it also changes our relationship to places.

So I narrow it down to a spot. I tell my lit professor I'm going to miss my nine a.m. class—she understands—and go down to the apartment I still think of as home and take Sammy to school. It seemed unusual at first to decide to live in the dorms, but I petitioned to be in an international dorm, and the fact that I'm surrounded by people from all over the world seems to make up for the fact that I'm still twenty blocks from home. I only moved out three weeks ago, so I don't think Sammy's even missing me yet.

He's quiet as we walk from the subway to the school—aware of the anniversary, I think, but not of its full meaning. I wonder what's going to happen when he's older, what parts of 9/11 he's going to remember.

After he's safely inside his classroom, I leave the building and stand outside, in that gap on Sixth Avenue between the lower school and the upper school. As the time nears, a few more people stop and hover, regathering. I wonder about Marisol, and where she is. I wonder if some of the other people here were also here a year ago. I find I can't remember them, I was so caught up in getting to Sammy and finding my mother.

A year ago, I wouldn't let myself turn around, look back. Now I join everyone else in looking at the space. Silent, we look at what isn't there. We are doing our own acts of retracing, so much more complicated than the retracing of steps. We are retracing the lines and windows that are no longer there. We are rebuilding from our memory, trying to do with our eyes open what we usually do with our eyes closed.

At 8:46, bells ring out. And I think, *This is the moment I wasn't here. This is the moment of what I didn't see.* And then, when the time comes, *This was when I came out here. I stood over there. This was when.*

I still cannot hear a siren without fearing the monumental. I cannot help noticing the airplanes over the city, which I never paid attention to before. Most of the time I manage to forget to be afraid. But sometimes I think, *This could be it,* and I move forward anyway.

It crosses my mind every day. Sometimes it will be a story I hear on the radio. Sometimes I'll be walking and will look downtown. And other times it will be like I am seeing it out of the corner of my eye.

I feel emptier this morning. That empty space goes inside. It is not the whole story, but it is a part of it. And the rest of the story is: We love and we feel and we try and we hope.

I can't help it—I find Sammy's new third-grade classroom and peek in through the window. I see him at his desk, doing something with pipe cleaners. He isn't smiling—instead he's concentrating in that complete, unembarrassed way that kids have. I stay there for a minute or two, watching.

This has to be part of the day, too.

ANNIVERSARY
Peter

I said, "Are you sure September 11th is an appropriate day for a second date?"

And he said, "I'll see you on Wednesday."

But the conversation didn't end there, as it once might have. He paused and said, "Who else would you want to spend it with?"

And he's right. Probably Claire, but she's in New York right now. So, yes, Jasper.

I pointed out that it wasn't even our real anniversary—only the anniversary of the night we were supposed to go out. He laughed into the phone and told me that was great, because now he didn't have to bring flowers. I pressed the phone to my ear, heard his breathing after the sentence was over. I waited for him to say something else, because if I wait long enough, he always does. He's like Claire in that way. Whereas I can stay in silences for hours.

We decided that he'd come to visit me in Boston, so I'm waiting for him at South Station. I spent most of the morning— the time I wasn't in classes—reading the papers, reading all of the takes on what 9/11 means, one year later. I still feel like I should be at home. Maybe standing outside Tower Records. Or with my family.

I haven't seen Jasper since Claire's party in May, but it feels like I have. When I find him in the terminal, we hug, not kiss. And before we do anything else, we call Claire, who picks up on the first ring and tells us she was hoping we'd call. She says she's been looking at the photos of the lights, creating her own little remembrance ceremony. She wishes she were with us, and we wish she were with us, too. Not that we don't want to be alone with each other. But today, now, we'd also love to be with her.

"So," Jasper says once we've hung up, "what should we do?"

I've only been here a few weeks; all I know are cheap restaurants and record stores. I take him to Newbury Comics and buy him the Now It's Overhead CD because he says he's never heard of them. I launch into this whole history of Saddle Creek records, then cut myself off, because it's not really something he would be interested in.

"I don't really have sophisticated musical taste," he tells me. "But I'd like to."

That's good enough for me.

Next stop is Bertucci's for dinner. It's a little too crowded, a little too loud. And even though the papers and newscasts have been full of it, everyday life doesn't seem to have stopped much to remember a year ago. Not in Boston, at least. I'm worried that we're not talking, that we haven't had a chance to talk, and that maybe we're going to end up much better at emailing than being with each other in person.

"This is strange," he says, and I don't know whether he's talking about us or the restaurant or the day. I wait, and he goes on. "I saw Amanda on my way to class this morning—you know, the girl I tried to give blood with? I don't think I've seen her in at least half a year, but today of all days, I bump into her. And she tells me she was just thinking about me—she's been thinking about me a lot lately, because I was a part of that day for her. And I understood what she was saying, but the weird thing was that I hadn't really thought of her at all. I think of you, and Claire, and even Mitchell and his party. It's like, for most people, that day is about what happened on that specific day, but for me it's become about what happened right after. It's not what I saw, but it's about who I shared it with. Is it like that for you?"

"The truth?" I ask.   .

He smiles. "Yeah, the truth."

"The truth is that I don't know. Because you *were* a part of that day for me. I was so excited that morning when I woke up, about going out with you. I mean, I was excited about the Dylan album, too, but mostly about you. I was thinking about you when I picked out what to wear, and I was thinking about you when I got on the subway, and I was probably thinking about you while I was waiting for Tower to open. And even after it all happened, I remember thinking that I had to email you, that I had to make sure you were okay, that it meant something that such a big event got in our way."

"And then, of course, I was a complete asshole to you," Jasper says.

"No," I say. "You weren't. That's how you're remembering it, but you weren't. When you say things like that—" I stop.

"What?"

"When you say things like that, I wonder if we're here now because you feel bad. You know, about the first date. That you're only doing this to be nice."

That gets a laugh. "I think that's the first time anyone's accused me of doing something just to be nice." He moves forward so that his knees are touching my knees under the table. "I promise you, this isn't about then. It's about now."

I press my knees back into his. "Fine, then."

"We have an understanding?"

"I believe we do."

We talk about how strange it is to be away from New York. We both called our parents this morning, as if it were Mother's Day or a birthday. There wasn't much to say, except to acknowledge what we should already know.

"I remember on that day," I say, "one of the city officials—it wasn't Giuliani, but someone else—anyway, when he was asked what people should do, he said that everyone should go home and give their kids a hug. And while I understood why he was saying that, part of me wanted to say, dude, you should *always* go home and give your kids a hug. It shouldn't take the World Trade Center falling to inspire that."

Jasper shakes his head. "I'm not sure my dad would've

gotten the message anyway. But you know what? I'm okay with that."

I know I should be planning the next thing to say—I know I should be trying to tap into all the relationship politics, the signs and signals, that could be at the table. But instead I just talk and listen. And he just talks and listens. Maybe in the end that's all we need. Talking and listening.

At the end of the meal I say, "Hey, do you want to come back to my dorm room and watch *Cabaret?*"

He pushes back his chair in surprise and says, "Whoa, this is so *Sliding Doors.*"

"I actually think it's more like *Groundhog Day,*" I reply. And then I explain: In *Sliding Doors,* the whole idea is that every choice you make, and every single thing that happens to you, changes the trajectory of your life, and once you are put on that trajectory, there is no way back. But *Groundhog Day*—which, I tell him, also happens to be a much better movie—says the opposite. It says if you mess up or make the wrong choice, you just have to keep at it until you do it right.

"So we've been stuck in the same day for a year?" Jasper says. And I know what he's thinking—that the day in question is September 11th, which would be somewhat lunatic, because that day is about much, much more than our date going right.

So I shake my head. "No. The fact that it all happens in one day in *Groundhog Day* is a comedic conceit."

"Oh, sorry. Silly me."

I swat at him with my napkin. He fends me off with his water glass. Water spills everywhere.

"What I'm saying," I continue, "is that the trajectory can loop around. If we want it to."

He leans into the table and presses his knees against mine again.

"Do we want it to?" he asks.

And I say, "Hey, do you want to come back to my dorm room and watch *Cabaret?*"

This time, the TV stays off.

This time, we sleep in the same bed.

"You have a little more body hair now," I say.

He kisses me, then whispers in my ear, "No, I don't."

MARCH 19, 2003
Claire

It's a similar dread, a similar fear, a similar sadness, only in reverse. Instead of reaction, the dread comes in the anticipation. Instead of aftershocks, the fear comes from the assemblage. Instead of the devastating After, the sadness springs from the devastating Before.

I know we're going to start a war. I know it as soon as the president starts talking about it. I know it as soon as they start linking Iraq to 9/11. I know it when they start conjuring doomsday as the alternative.

It's a similar helplessness, only in reverse. It's not that I can't undo what's happened, but that I can't stop something from happening. We have our protests, but Dick Cheney doesn't care what a hundred thousand people in San Francisco have to say. We hound members of Congress, but our money doesn't talk as much as that of the other forces. We argue with our friends, but our friends are powerless, too.

I don't want to watch it happening, but I have to. I have to turn on the television and read the papers, because we all need to be witnessing. I thought, for a time, that we understood that we are a part of the world. And many of us do, just not the people in charge of our government, the people who less than a majority of us voted for. We are losing the human scale.

The night the war begins, I cry more than I did on 9/11. Jasper and Peter are home together for spring break, and they come over and try to cheer me up by reading me things from the paper that show me that humanity is alive and well. Animal rescues. Families reunited after fifty years. A town of four hundred people chipping in to save its fire department. I love Jasper and Peter when they do this, and I love those people in the world. But still I despair.

We keep waiting for the next attack, and then we go and make the next attack.

I wish someone had taken George Bush and made him spend the night in Union Square, surrounded by the candles, surrounded by the dead. I wish there was a way to make him feel the depth of that loss. I wish he had been forced to spend a night in Baghdad, talking to the people there, before he bombed it.

There were lessons, I want to tell him. *Don't you understand?*

It's a similar sleeplessness, only in reverse. I used to wander at night to connect myself to the city. I searched desperately to find out what I could do. It was never enough, but it was something. Now I still want to know what I can do. It's never enough, and it feels like nothing.

An eye for an eye. Blindness.

I believe we're better than this.

Jasper and Peter stay up with me. Together we head into

the West Village, then cross over to the East Village. I know so many more people now, but it feels right to be with them. I hold them dear like I hold my mother and Sammy dear. I know I can count on them—meaning, they are as reliable as the simple sequence of 1-2-3.

"If I hadn't met you," Jasper says, "I probably wouldn't even know there was a war happening."

"If I hadn't met you," Peter says to Jasper, "I probably wouldn't even know what the songs meant."

"And if I hadn't met you," I say to them both, "I would've wondered if it was all in my head. My whole life, in my head."

We are in another part of the city, in another part of another year. Our thoughts, I'm sure, travel to different things—how difficult long-distance relationships are, how scary war is, how close the summer is already seeming, how amazing it is that friendships can become so full that you can't imagine what your life was like before them. We talk and we talk, and then we talk some more, until we are back in my dorm room. My roommate is home in Ghana for the break, but even though the second bed is open, we all lie on my bed, Jasper leaning into Peter, me leaning into them both. There's no way for them to take away my sadness, but they can make sure I am not empty of all the other feelings.

"I honestly thought we were going to be better," I tell them. "After what happened. As a country."

"I don't know if you can change a country," Jasper says. "You can only change the people."

And here we are, so different from who we were on September 10th. And also different from who we were on the 11th. And the 12th. And yesterday. Sometimes you see the before/after. And sometimes it's as soft as saying hello.

It is so comfortable, just the three of us on our bed in our room. It would be so easy to want to confine us to this. To unplug the TV. To turn off the computer. To only look at the sky whenever we looked out the window.

But that's not the way we live now. Every day, we choose not to live that way. Instead we have each other as we try to navigate the world.

We fall asleep in my bed, a tangle of three. It is the sweetest feeling, to be nestled between the two of them, their smiles fading into sleep, their arms enfolding me and each other. This is the antidote.

The next morning, we go to get breakfast together. As we are walking through Washington Square Park, Peter looks downtown, at the empty space.

He doesn't have to tell us to wait. We all stop. The sun is newly in the sky, and the city is like a quiet house, still ours.

For ten minutes, we keep watch over the sky and the skyline.

This is what a memorial is:

Standing still, staring at something that isn't there.

Author's Note

Some of the phrases in this book are taken directly from emails I sent to friends on 9/11 and afterwards. I was in the rooftop cafeteria of my office (roughly twenty blocks north of the World Trade Center) for most of the events of 9/11, but every now and then I felt the need to go back to my desk and write everything down. On that day and immediately after, I never would have thought I would someday write a novel about what was happening; words seemed an inadequate way to capture it, and facts dwarfed any attempts at fiction. It was only years later that this book began in earnest. I approached it with much trepidation, but was fueled by the fact that there haven't been as many novels about this time as I'd imagined there would be, and also by the fact that as time goes on, readers (especially younger ones) will have less and less firsthand experience of what it was like to be in New York in those hours and days and months. I genuinely can't imagine forgetting any of it, but I also have come to realize that history moves on, and while the meaning of that day changes in the context of what happens afterwards, the experience of the day needs to be preserved with as much immediacy as we can give it. For me, it is still one of the most harrowing and inspiring days I've ever lived through. Harrowing for what happened, and inspiring for how we held on.

There's no way to acknowledge all the people who factored into this book because I'd have to retrace all the people whose paths I intersected with in those hours and days and months, from the people who were in 555 Broadway with me to the friends who took me in when I couldn't get home to the people I saw days later in Brooklyn to the friends I marched in an anti-war rally with four years later. So many conversations went into my thoughts about 9/11, and I'm sure I drew on many of them here. In particular, the line that Claire's mother says on page 16 about not being able to comprehend something like 9/11 was actually something said by my friend Karen Nagel on that day. Thank you to Cindy Bullens for letting me borrow her song.

This book was written in many places, including my apartment, my parents' house, my friend Eliot's apartment, and my friends Mike and Mireia's house on Cape Cod. Thanks to all of them (and not just for their dwellings). Thanks as always to my family and friends for supporting me in ways big and small. And thanks, too, to my niece Paige and my nephew Matthew, whose ages on 9/11/01 (twenty-one months and not yet born, respectively) helped make me realize why it's good to write these things down.

Once more, I owe thanks to Allison Wortche, Melissa

166

Nelson, Noreen Marchisi, and everyone at Knopf. Most of all, I owe thanks to my editor, Nancy Hinkel—I am ever in debt to your twisted point of view and your questioning eyebrows. I couldn't have written this book for anyone else.

ALSO BY DAVID LEVITHAN

BOY MEETS BOY

An ALA Top Ten Best Book for Young Adults
A Lambda Literary Award Winner

★ "[A] breakthrough book."   —*Booklist*, Starred
"A refreshing, offbeat romance."   —*Publishers Weekly*

THE REALM OF POSSIBILITY

An ALA Top Ten Best Book for Young Adults
A New York Public Library Book for the Teen Age

★ "All teenagers will find themselves, their relationships, and their attitudes toward life, love, and the pursuit of happiness somewhere in these poems."
—*Kirkus Reviews*, Starred

ARE WE THERE YET?

An ALA Best Book for Young Adults

"Slyly witty, poignant, and lyrical."   —*The Bulletin*

WIDE AWAKE

A New York Public Library Book for the Teen Age

★ "Levithan's latest reaches out to shake readers awake, showing them how each person's life touches another, and another, until ultimately history is made."   —*Booklist*, Starred

HOW THEY MET, AND OTHER STORIES

A Book Sense Children's Pick

★ "The author is a master of texture and detail, managing a deft and eloquent exploration of feeling. . . . Each richly imagined story will tap familiar veins of longing, memory, and anticipation." —*The Bulletin*, Starred

BOOKS BY RACHEL COHN AND DAVID LEVITHAN

NICK & NORAH'S INFINITE PLAYLIST

An ALA Best Book for Young Adults
An ALA Top Ten Quick Pick

★ "An emotional, passionate, cathartic, and ultimately hopeful night of wandering, music, and incipient love. . . . Electric, sexy . . . and genuinely poignant." —*The Bulletin*, Starred

NAOMI AND ELY'S NO KISS LIST

An ALA Rainbow List Selection for GLBTQ Content for Youth

"A brilliant tour-de-force—funny, sweet, sly, and sexy."   —*Kirkus Reviews*
"A witty and highly entertaining exploration of love, friendship, and misunderstanding."   —*School Library Journal*

Coming soon!

DASH & LILY'S BOOK OF DARES